Black Rose

By

Alex Lukeman

Copyright 2015 by Alex Lukeman

http://www.alexlukeman.com

Ring around the rosie,
A pocket full of posies,
Ashes, ashes,
All fall down.

Prologue

Constantinople: 541 C.E.

The city was dying.

Smoke and ash from the funeral pyres drifted from a metallic grey sky, covering everything with a layer of fine black soot, even the dome of the emperor's magnificent church. The dead and dying lay in rotting heaps throughout the city. The stench reached to the heavens.

A lone figure made his way through the deserted streets, a rag held over his mouth and nose. He stepped around a decomposing corpse. Fat, green flies swarmed around the body, crawling over the dead man's eyes and into his open mouth. The fingers of the corpse were black and rotten.

Andreas cursed the day he'd come here. At first it had been good. His reputation as a maker of good copper pots had spread and in a few months he'd started to earn decent money. Then the plague had come.

Some said it came from Egypt, some said from the underworld itself. Wherever it came from, there were not so many people now to wonder about it. Those that were left had given up any pretense of morality. They copulated in the streets, drank until they were unconscious, attacked the weak and defenseless. The thought made Andreas feel for the comforting shape of the dagger he kept under his tunic.

A sudden headache made him stumble. He felt thirsty, tired, and his stomach was uneasy. His throat burned. Fear rippled through his body. He lifted his tunic and searched for the outward signs of the disease, the black patches that spread like poisonous flowers over the doomed.

He found nothing and breathed a sigh of relief. It was probably just a headache. Who wouldn't be tired? He couldn't remember when he'd last had a good night's sleep or eaten a good meal. He'd been hiding with his wife and son. They should have left the city while they were still healthy but his wife had been afraid and now it was too late. The emperor had ordered the gates sealed before he'd died and no one had countered the order..

Hunger and the cries of his child had driven him into the streets. His destination was a bakery in the next alley. Andreas turned the corner and saw three men standing drunk in front of the shop. Through the open door of the shop, he saw the baker lying on the floor. The stones were stained red around him. Beyond the body, there was still a single loaf of bread on one of the shelves.

One of the men saw Andreas approaching and nudged his comrades. He raised a wineskin to his lips, swallowed and threw the empty skin to the side.

"What do you want?" he said. His words were slurred.

Andreas felt for his dagger. "Bread. A loaf of bread for my family."

"Go away," the man said. "This is our shop, our bread."

The second man peered at him through bloodshot eyes. "That's a nice tunic you're wearing," he said. "Give it to me."

Andreas drew his dagger. "All I want is bread for my child. Let me pass."

"Ooh," the leader said. "A pig sticker."

Suddenly the three men didn't seem so drunk anymore. The leader drew a long curved blade from behind his back. The second man drew a dagger from his belt. The third reached for a stout cudgel standing against the wall of the shop.

Andreas coughed, a deep. racking cough that shook his body in a violent spasm. He tasted blood, a sudden rush of warm liquid inside his mouth. He bent over and vomited a thick, red stream onto the cobbles.

The three men backed away in fear. Without another word, they turned and ran.

Andreas wiped his lips. He retched again, then staggered into the shop, stepped over the body of the baker and took the stale loaf from the shelf.

My poor family, he thought. *What will you do when I'm gone?*

In the broad central square of the city, the funeral pyres burned.

CHAPTER 1

The biological weapons lab where Kim Bong Cha worked was deep inside an abandoned gold mine in North Korea's Pinandok Mountain Range, invisible to the spy satellites of the West. Cha had been given a lot of responsibility for her twenty-seven years. Her superiors often praised her dedication. It was hard to find much to criticize about her, even in a society where criticism was a way of life.

If Cha had a flaw, it was bad judgment in men. She lived with a petty criminal named Hyo who made his living smuggling recordings of foreign television programs out of China and into the Democratic People's Republic. When he pulled off one of his deals there was good money and Hyo was happy. Hyo was always happy with money in his pocket and enough to drink. But the money never lasted and he would become surly and abusive until he found his next big score. Now he'd found it and he needed Cha to make it possible.

Hyo had been urgent this morning as Cha was getting ready to go to work, even scary. She could smell the first drink of the day on his breath. There was menace in his voice when he'd told her what he wanted.

She'd argued.

"Hyo, it's dangerous. If I'm caught, they'll take me to one of the camps."

"You won't be caught. All you have to do is open the door."

It was his promise that they'd use the money to escape to the South that persuaded Cha to do what he'd asked. She'd always wanted to go to the South, away from the grim paranoia and poverty of the North. The forbidden television programs made it look like a magical place where everyone was happy and wealthy.

She looked at the clock on the wall. *Almost time*, she thought.

Cha was part of a team responsible for creating new biological weapons using genetic mutations in bacteria and viruses. She was working with a sample identified only as E495. At 200 X magnification, E495 looked like a rod-shaped clump of safety pins entwined in sticky strands and filaments. The bumps and filaments told her that the sample was from the family of *Yersinia Pestis*, bubonic plague. She'd worked with plague before but she'd never seen a sample like this. It was a mutation resurrected from the dead and given new life with the best genetic enhancements science could devise.

North Korea's scientists had manipulated genomes from the teeth of three skeletons unearthed in Turkey to bring it back to life. The sample under Cha's microscope hadn't come from a skeleton, though. It had been taken from the blood of a rat living in her laboratory.

The rat wouldn't be among the living for long.

The most common form of bubonic plague was well understood, the famous Black Death that had ravaged Europe and London in the Middle Ages. It responded to modern antibiotics and was seldom fatal, if caught in time. But E495 came from victims of an extinct strain that had swept through the Byzantine Empire in the sixth century. It was different from the common varieties. It always emerged as the pneumonic form, becoming airborne soon after the host was infected. All the rats and monkeys used for tests had died or were dying. They coughed and sneezed a lot before they died. The fatality rate was one hundred percent. So far, E495 had resisted all efforts to find a cure.

Cha tried not to think about why her country wanted to experiment with the lethal plagues and viruses she saw on a daily basis. *It's not my concern*, she told herself. She often told herself that things were not her concern. In the People's Democratic Republic of North Korea, the words were a mantra of survival.

Doctor Park would make the final evaluation, but she could see that this particular sample was different. The shape of the deadly bacillus was highly unusual. The bacteria were mutating. She made a final note, removed the specimen from her microscope and placed it back in its secure container. Once inside the container, the plague was isolated and safe.

She got up from the bench where she'd been working and made her way to the storage cabinet where Level 4 pathogens were kept. Hoses connected to her pressurized suit trailed in loops behind her from a rack overhead. The Level 4 vaults contained a collection of the deadliest infectious agents in the world and there had been many deaths at the facility over the years, though most of those had been prisoners used in experimental trials. The biohazard suit kept her alive when she was in the room.

She placed the sealed container of E495 in the storage locker, closed the door and activated a system that exchanged and sterilized the air inside. It was essential to purify the air because the storage vault could be accessed from outside the room where she worked without entering the lab itself. Only secure containers went into that locker, brought in from the outside or taken away in specially constructed transport boxes. The containment laboratory where she worked was for when the killers were out of their cage.

She'd been suited up for half an hour and was exhausted. The air entering her suit did little to keep her cool. It was difficult enough to work with something that would kill her if she gave it a chance. The stress was made worse by the confines of the suit. It was hard work.

Exiting the lab was a tedious process. She went through a pressurized airlock and into a decontamination room where chemical sprays soaked her suit. Then she entered a vacuum room where she could undress. After that came a series of stinging showers that smelled of more chemicals. She hated the showers. They dried out her hair and irritated her skin. Still naked, she went through another airlock into a room where she dressed. After one more airlock she was outside again, breathing normally.

Usually there were people here in the outer room, but not tonight. She'd stayed late, claiming the pressure of work. Everyone was gone except for the guards in the halls. From the outside, the door to the laboratory could only be opened with the proper card and biometric authentication. From the inside, anyone could press down on the handle. She walked over to the locked door leading into the rest of the underground complex.

Bong Cha looked at her watch and remembered Hyo's instructions. He'd been adamant, specific, making her repeat what he'd said.

14

"You open the door at 7:20 tonight. 7:20 exactly. You understand? Someone will come in. Don't talk to him. Show him where the containment locker is. Go home. That's all you have to do."

"There are cameras. What if someone sees? What if I'm caught?"

"It's taken care of, no one will see. Look, this is our chance. My cousin is waiting for us in Seoul. He's the one who told me about this man, it's alright."

"Your cousin is mafia."

"My cousin is a businessman, that's all."

"The locker is restricted. What about the guards?"

"Don't worry about it. Look, I told you, it's all taken care of. The guards won't be a problem. Just show him where the samples are stored, then leave. Don't argue."

"Yes, Hyo."

She looked at her watch. It was 7:20. She opened the door and took an involuntary step away.

Three men stood there, not one. They were dressed in black. They had black masks pulled over their faces. One of them had a pack on his back. Two of them held assault rifles. The third had one of the specialized transport carriers in his hand.

"Hello, Cha," the first man said.

He drew a knife and in one, quick motion slashed it across her throat. Bong Cha's blood sprayed out across her attacker, across the door, the wall. She tried to speak, to scream, but only blood bubbled from her mouth. She clutched at her throat with both hands, stumbled backward and died.

"Move," the leader said. His voice was guttural, low. "Get the locker open and take everything. Be careful."

The second man stood guard with his assault rifle. The third went to the locker and opened the door. There were sixteen samples inside, neatly labeled. With great care, he began transferring the contents into the container he'd brought with him.

"Hurry up," the leader said.

The man at the locker closed the lid of the transport container and locked it down.

"Done."

The leader set his rifle down, un-shouldered his pack, opened the flap and reached in. He flipped a switch. Inside the pack, a digital counter began ticking down a four minute count in red numbers.

"Four minutes," he said. He left the pack on the floor and picked up his rifle. One man took the container and the three left the room.

Behind them, Bong Cha lay sprawled and graceless, ugly in death. She would never know what she had done by opening that door.

It was just as well.

CHAPTER 2

Elizabeth Harker had been hand-picked for her job as Director of the Project by President Rice. Rice was determined that he wasn't going to be one of those leaders who ended up like the fairy tale emperor with no clothes. It was easy to find people who told him what he wanted to hear, harder to find someone who'd tell him what he needed to hear. He'd found that person in Elizabeth. Not many people knew who she was or what her unit did. The Project operated in the shadows, as much out of public view as the dark side of the moon.

Nick Carter and Selena Connor sat on the couch in front of her desk. Nick had spent years in Marine Recon and led the Project's field team, all Special Forces vets except Selena. She'd come from the civilian world, with a unique mix of abilities that balanced the hard military background of the others.

Selena had a gift for ancient languages and spoke a dozen modern languages with ease. She knew martial arts and had used them more than once since Harker had recruited her. Since she'd joined the Project, she'd begun to pick up some of the lethal skills Nick and the others had spent years refining in the military.

The third member of the team was Lamont Cameron. He sat in a chair near the couch. His looks were marred by a thin, pink scar that stood out against his coffee-colored skin. It ran over his right eye and down the side of his nose, a souvenir of Iraq. Lamont was a former Navy SEAL. He had blue eyes that missed little, a genetic gift from his Ethiopian ancestors.

"Have you heard anything from Ronnie?" Elizabeth asked.

Ronnie Peete was the fourth member of her field team. He'd been badly wounded during a recent mission in the Philippines and gone back to Arizona after leaving the hospital. He'd told Nick he was going home to the Navajo reservation for a healing ceremony. That had been two weeks ago.

"I talked to him yesterday," Nick said. "He didn't say when he was coming back."

"All right. Bring him up to date when he gets here."

Elizabeth got to the point of the meeting.

"What do you know about North Korea's biological warfare program?" she said.

Nick rubbed the scar on his left ear, where a Chinese bullet had clipped the earlobe. His eyes were smoky gray, with gold flecks in them. His black hair was cut short. He was six feet tall and weighed in at just under two hundred. He wore a gray jacket that matched his eyes. A slight bulge under the jacket signaled a shoulder holster. Everyone in the Project went armed at all times.

"I don't know anything about it," he said, "but it figures they'd have one. I hope you're not thinking of sending us to North Korea."

"No," she said. "I'm sending you to Hong Kong."

"That's comforting."

"We have time to hit the malls?" Lamont asked. "I always wanted one of those silk suits."

"It's too early for the jokes, Lamont."

"Sorry, Director."

Elizabeth tapped a file on her desktop with her finger. "This is a transcript of an NSA intercept between the head of North Korea's bio warfare program and the Vice-Chairman of their National Defense Commission. He's second in command to the Supreme Leader. Their top general."

"What were they talking about?" Nick asked.

"There's been a security breach at their biological weapons lab."

"What kind of a breach?" Selena asked.

She wore dark blue slacks and a loose top that matched. A SIG-Sauer .40 caliber pistol in a quick draw holster at her waist added a black accent to her casual look. The outfit complimented her violet eyes and reddish-blonde hair. Selena was a woman who drew second looks wherever she went.

Harker said, "The People's Democratic Republic is working with some very nasty bugs. You know about bubonic plague?"

"I know it killed a lot of people back in the Middle Ages. Don't you get lumps under your arms and in the groin? Black spots?"

"That's right. It takes over the lymph nodes and destroys the immune system, then spreads to the organs. Death is usually within one to two weeks if left untreated. There's a septicemic variety that bleeds under the skin and turns parts black. That's why it was called the Black Death in the Middle Ages. It affects coagulation. You get to watch your fingers turn black and rot before you die."

Lamont looked at his hands.

"How is it spread?" Nick asked.

"Usually by a flea bite but there are other ways as well. There's a pneumonic form that infects through a cough or a sneeze. One of the things that keeps the World Health Organization up at night is the fear that a plague epidemic would go airborne."

Harker paused and picked up her pen, a black Mont Blanc. She tapped it three times on her desk. "Our North Korean friends have developed a super strain of airborne plague. We think they weaponized it with aerosols."

Nick shook his head. "What's the matter with these people?" He looked at her. "You're going to tell me some of this stuff has gone missing, aren't you?"

She nodded. "That's what the conversation we intercepted was about. The Korean lab is a Level 4 bio hazard facility. That's the highest level of containment. Ten days ago a technician let several men into the laboratory. They killed her and the guards and took containers with samples of the new bacteria. Then they planted charges and left. It was a well-executed op, military in precision. When the balloon went up the lab was destroyed and part of the mountain collapsed on top of it. That's the only good thing about this. The People's Republic won't be making any more of that bug for a while."

"How do they know what happened if everything was destroyed?"

"Video records of the whole thing. Security cameras recorded images from the containment labs in a separate building."

Nick waited.

"I met with the President and DCI Hood this morning," Elizabeth said. "They want us to handle a delicate mission."

"We don't usually do delicate," Nick said.

"It's a political bomb. Rice doesn't want to use Langley or any of the regular JSOC units, in case it doesn't work out."

Nick sighed. "What does he want us to do?"

"We need to know exactly what the North Koreans had. The chief scientist of Pyongyang's biological warfare program is a man named Kim Jung-Hun. He almost never leaves North Korea but he's attending an international conference in Hong Kong this weekend. He wants to defect. In return for asylum he's willing to give us details about their program."

"Whoa," Nick said, "that's a big fish."

"That's exactly what he is and the President wants to land him," Elizabeth said.

Nick said, "You want us to go pick him up."

Elizabeth nodded. "It's not going to be easy. I'm sending you and Lamont. Kim will be well guarded at all times. We only have a two day window and then he'll be back in North Korea. You'll have support for the extraction. But if something goes wrong before that, you're on your own. I can't protect you."

"How are we supposed to get him out?"

"A boat will be available for you courtesy of MI-6, once you have Kim."

"And how are we supposed to scoop him up?"

Elizabeth smiled. "That's up to you, Nick. Use your imagination."

CHAPTER 3

The black chop of the East China Sea slapped against the hull of boat. Nick braced himself against the constant, unpleasant motion. A black wool watch cap and thick jacket kept out some of the dank, night chill. Thick fog muffled the sound of their engine. Droplets of moisture lay like the touch of an obsessive lover over every surface of the boat.

The boat was old and slow. A tall, open wheelhouse did nothing to protect from the tendrils of fog reaching everywhere. Tiny streams of water trickled down the glass faces of the dimly lit gauges on the control console. The old style helm was slick and his left hand ached from gripping the wheel. The last two fingers had been broken by a sadistic Cuban policeman and continued to give him trouble. Nick tried to see through the fog and hoped they didn't run into one of the Chinese patrol boats that moved in these waters.

They had succeeded in grabbing Kim Jung-Hun in Hong Kong but it had been messy, with three of Kim's minders dead. By now all of China's security services were looking for the mouse-like man shivering in the cabin below. The Chinese and North Koreans would do everything they could to get Kim back. If they couldn't get him back, Nick was certain they'd settle for killing him.

Lamont came up from below deck and joined Nick in the wheelhouse. He scanned the impenetrable fog with night vision binoculars.

"Can't see a damn thing," Lamont said. The fog sucked up the sound of his voice. He put the binoculars down.

"How's our guest?" Nick said.

"Seasick. Barfing in a bucket. It stinks down there. I had to get some fresh air."

"They'll have figured it out by now," Nick said. "Someone will be out here looking for us."

Lamont grunted. There wasn't any point in worrying about all the things that could go wrong.

"Better get the RPG ready just in case," Nick said. The grenade launcher lay in an open box on the floor of the wheelhouse.

Lamont pulled it out of the box, loaded a round.

"All set," Lamont said. "Let's hope we don't need it. Not a lot of use against a patrol boat."

"Better than nothing."

"Yeah."

For a few minutes both men were silent, the only sound the muffled rhythm of the engine and the water against the hull.

"The fog is starting to thin," Nick said. "I don't think we'll have cover much longer."

"How far to the extraction point?" Lamont asked. They were headed for a rendezvous with a helicopter from an American Wasp class amphibious assault carrier.

"Another ten minutes," Nick said.

The fog clung to the gauges. Nick wiped droplets away with his right hand.

"Still plenty of fuel."

They both heard the sound at the same time.

"Engines. Big ones," Lamont said.

Nick cut the throttle and they drifted on the black water. Wisps of fog swirled around them. The sound seemed close.

"Maybe it's a fishing boat," Lamont said.

Nick pointed. "I don't think so," he said.

The sharp prow of a patrol vessel emerged from the gray as both boats entered a clear patch in the fog bank. The Chinese boat was long and lethal looking and bristling with guns. Nick rammed the throttles forward. A bright searchlight found them as they fled back into fog.

"Just our luck," Lamont said.

"That's a Shanghai II class," Nick said. "Obsolete, but she can do thirty knots. Dual 37s and 25s for the big stuff and heavy machine guns. They decide to start shooting, they can turn this tub into toothpicks in about ten seconds."

Nick steered deeper into the fog and throttled down.

Behind them they could hear shouts and alarms blaring, then silence.

The two vessels drifted in the fog.

"I never did like playing hide and seek," Lamont said.

"Get our guest up here. We may have to get off fast. I'll see if our ride is here yet, " Nick said. He adjusted his headpiece and turned on the transponder that identified him as friendly. Now that they'd been spotted, there was no need to stay dark.

"Raven One, this is Tango. Do you copy? Over."

His headpiece crackled.

"Tango, this is Raven One. We've got you. Looks like you've got company. What is your status?"

"Raven One, we've got a Chinese patrol on our ass. They've got anti-aircraft guns. Watch yourself."

"Copy, Tango. No problemo. Stay alive for five."

"Copy that."

Lamont went down to the tiny cabin and emerged a moment later with their charge. He was a small man, dressed in a shapeless brown suit. He clutched a briefcase in his hands and looked frightened. Nick couldn't blame him. If the North Koreans managed to get their hands on him, they would feed him alive to a pack of hungry dogs.

They drifted out of the thinning fog. Ahead, the sea was clear and dark. Stars shone overhead. Seconds later the Chinese boat emerged from the fog bank a bare thirty yards away. Their engines throttled up. A searchlight swung across the black water and pinned them in a bright, white glare. Nick watched the guns coming to bear.

"Lamont."

"I'm on it."

Lamont lifted the launcher and fired. The round struck the bridge and detonated in a bright, orange burst of flame. The Chinese craft slewed to port. Nick pushed the throttles ahead and spun the wheel to turn back toward the fog bank. Maneuverability was the only advantage he had. They churned to the right as cannon fire found the spot they'd just been. The patrol boat was burning where the grenade had hit. Lamont loaded another round and fired again, striking forward of the gun crews. Two bodies hurled into the air. The 25mm cannon on the foredeck hammered away at them, sending gouts of water into the air.

The Chinese machine guns opened up. Nick and Lamont hit the deck. Bullets stitched across the boat, smashed the control console and marched across the chest of Kim Jung-Hun. His briefcase slid across the deck as he fell. Nick reached up and spun the wheel. Shells from the 25mm gun struck aft and pieces of the trawler flew into the air. The engine screamed and shook itself apart and died with a final sound of tortured metal. The boat began to settle fast by the stern.

Nick heard the sound of rotors through the heavy explosions of the Chinese guns. An SH-60B Seahawk appeared, coming in low and hot a hundred feet off the water. The Chinese gunners swung around and began to fire, rows of bright tracers streaming toward the chopper. As Nick watched, two hellfire missiles shot from the aircraft.

The missiles lifted the Chinese ship partway out of the water and broke it in two. A thick column of water shot into the night sky. Nick grasped the railing of their sinking vessel as water rained down on him. The wave from the blast washed over the trawler. The patrol boat was gone from sight in less than a minute.

Kim lay dead on deck, his chest shredded and bloody from the bullets. His eyes were open. His face looked as though he'd seen something that had shocked him. Nick picked up the briefcase.

The stern was underwater, the boat listing to the side. Lamont stepped over the edge into the sea and began swimming away. Nick dove in after him. The boat turned bow up and slid under the roiling surface, trying to pull them in after it.

Overhead, the blades of the Seahawk beat patterns in the water. A circle of light found them. A hatch opened and a rescue basket descended.

Nick hoped they hadn't started a war.

CHAPTER 4

The Korean operation had put Major Igor
Kaminsky in a good mood. Action always did.
Kaminsky was a ranking field officer in *Zaslon*, a
special ops unit so secret and ruthless that the
Kremlin refused to admit it existed. He'd missed out
on the Ukraine, though it was still possible his elite
Spetsnaz unit would be sent there. *Or they might
send me to one of the Baltic territories*, he thought.
For Kaminsky and his masters, the Baltic states
were only temporarily independent entities. They all
had large ethnic Russian populations, with strong
internal movements that wanted to be part of *Novo
Rossiya*, the New Russia. His unit would be part of
any future operations in the Baltics.

In the meantime, he was enjoying the comfort
of a first class railroad car in a special train.
Kaminsky was on his way from Moscow to the
Sverdlovsk-19 Military Laboratory outside of
Yekaterinburg, on the eastern side of the Urals. Six
of his men rode in the car with him. An aluminum
case containing the North Korean samples sat on the
green plush of the seat next to him.

The attack on the research complex had gone
off without any problems. Security had been
surprisingly lax. Kaminsky had expected at least
twice as many guards but it seemed that the Great
Leader thought the hidden facility safe by virtue of
its secrecy and difficulty of access. The most
complicated part of the operation had been getting
himself and his men into the area and on site
without being detected. All of the men he'd chosen
for the mission had Asian features. Two spoke

fluent Korean. Multiple language skills were part of the basic requirements for a Spetsnaz operative.

Even scientists and guards had to eat. Kaminsky had driven right up to the gates in a produce delivery van, riding in back where his western features could not be seen. Killing the sentries at the guardhouse wasn't hard. Once inside the gates, the rest was easy.

It was too bad about the girl in the lab. She'd been pretty, until he'd cut her throat. There could be no trail back to her boyfriend and his Russian contact. Of course the boyfriend was dead as well. Perhaps they'd found each other in whatever Korean heaven they believed in, if they'd believed in anything except the illusion of the South.

The train was still on the western side of the Urals. Ahead, the mountains that separated European Russia from the rest of the country rose bleak and cold toward a winter sky filled with fast moving gray and black clouds. Snow lay thick along the railway embankment. A fresh storm was beginning, the wet flakes spattering against Kaminsky's window.

Kaminsky didn't mind the train ride. It made a pleasant change from the helicopters and noisy troop transports he was used to. He was thankful to whatever faceless bureaucrat had decided the train was the best way to send him and his package of bugs to the laboratory. Kaminsky reached over and patted the case next to him.

The train entered a long tunnel. The lights in the car flickered, then went dark. One of his men cursed.

"Lenin strikes again," someone said.

There was brief laughter, then silence in the car except for the rhythmic clacking of the wheels over the rails. In Russia, one accepted things like electrical failures as business as usual.

The train slowed, then stopped. It was pitch black in the tunnel. Major Kaminsky reached over to touch the case. It hadn't moved. Still, the darkness was unnerving.

Kaminsky heard the door at the end of the car open. *Good*, he thought, *now I'll find out what's holding us up. There had better be a good reason.*

He had time to see a red dot appear on his chest before a bullet drilled through his tunic and ended his thoughts about the train and everything else.

CHAPTER 5

Snow covered the gardens outside Elizabeth's office windows at Project headquarters. The room had a gas fireplace that radiated pleasant heat from behind a glass front. It looked like the real thing. A large, aging, orange tom cat named Burps lay curled up on the tile hearth in front of the flames. He snored. A damp spot on the tile showed where he drooled in his sleep.

"That cat makes a lot of noise," Lamont said.

"At least he's not burping or passing gas," Nick said.

Stephanie Willits was in the room with them. Harker's deputy handled the technology and communications end of Project operations. She was a legend among computer hackers, where she was known by her screen name, *Butterfly*. Stephanie used the big Crays in her computer room to tap into secure servers all over the world. Without her, Project operations would grind to a halt.

Selena sat next to Nick on the couch. She wore a diamond ring that sparkled in the light of the gas fire. Since they'd made the engagement official, the tension between them that always seemed to be part of their relationship had eased. Elizabeth was grateful for that. She had enough to worry about without having to deal with their personal problems on top of everything else. They still hadn't set a wedding date. She hoped it didn't turn into another problem.

"Let's get started." Elizabeth tapped her pen on her desk. "Selena has been translating the contents of Kim's briefcase. I've asked her to brief us on what she found."

"Most of it was the kind of thing you'd expect," Selena said. "Office memos, bureaucratic busy work, even an invitation to a birthday party."

"They have parties in North Korea?"

"Lamont..." Elizabeth's voice had a warning note in it.

"Sorry."

"The rest of it was notes and research that confirm what we learned from that intercept. North Korea has recreated a disease that killed twenty million people in the sixth century. It was called the Plague of Justinian, after the Roman Emperor who ruled Constantinople at the time. He was one of the victims."

"Twenty million is a lot of people," Lamont said.

"That was only the first time around," Elizabeth said. "It reappeared several times after that until it finally died out sometime in the eighth century. By then it had killed over a hundred million."

Lamont whistled.

"What makes it so lethal?" Nick asked.

"It's a variation of bubonic plague. The normal form is bad enough, but you can beat it with antibiotics if you catch it in time. This variation is one hundred percent fatal and it's airborne. That's the worst kind. Kim literally brought the disease back from the dead by manipulating genomes from victims dug up in Turkey. Then he tweaked it to make it resistant to all known drugs. There's no treatment, according to his notes. Apparently the Great Leader wasn't interested in finding one. Kim's lab was weaponizing it for use in an aerial spray, like they use in crop dusters. The thieves took live samples of the bacteria."

"Ah, hell," Lamont said.

"Yes."

Elizabeth picked up her Mont Blanc and tapped it on the desk. "It was an inside job. The woman who let the thieves in is dead and so is her boyfriend. The raid has the feel of a military op by someone's Special Forces. We don't know who took the samples yet. When we find out, our job is to get them back."

"You mind telling me how we're supposed to do that if it was taken by a government?" Nick asked. "We don't even know it was a government. It could have been terrorists."

"I don't think so. Neither does DCI Hood. The operation was too good, smooth as silk, in and out with everyone dead and they disappear. Terrorists aren't that sophisticated."

"Not yet," Lamont said. "Give them time."

"That's not a good thought," Selena said.

"If someone decides to unleash this thing, millions will die," Elizabeth said. "Garden variety Spanish Flu killed millions in 1918. This is much worse."

"So how do we find out who has it?" Nick asked.

"That's where I come in," Stephanie said. "Freddie is working on it right now."

Freddie was a maxed out Cray XT super computer that Stephanie had modified for greater power. This was the second one named Freddie. The first had been destroyed with the old Project headquarters. Steph had names for all of the computers, even her laptop. That one was named

Lily. Nick had caught Steph talking to them, more than once.

"I'm analyzing all the satellite and communications intelligence from the period leading up to the raid and after. When the program finishes running we'll know more."

"In the meantime there's something else I want to bring up," Elizabeth said. "The last year was rough. Lamont was out for a good part of it. Ronnie almost got killed and he's still not back. Lamont, you've been talking about retiring."

"I said I was thinking about it, I didn't say I was definitely going to do it. That dive shop I was looking at down in Florida got bought out from under me. I'm not ready for a rocking chair, not yet."

"I'm sorry about the shop, but I'm glad to know you're not leaving. My point is that we've been hampered by injuries and time down. I've been wondering if we should add a new member to the team. We could use more strength."

Her words were greeted by silence.

"Well? What do you think? Nick?"

"I think it would create problems."

"How so?"

"We work well together as we are. It's automatic. We understand each other. We add someone and it changes the dynamic. It could mess things up, especially when we know a mission is coming, like now."

"Or it could make things better," Elizabeth said. "There's always going to be a mission and never a good time to introduce someone new."

Nick looked at her. "I don't think it's a good idea. I can see it down the road, if someone decides they've had enough. But not now."

"He's right, Director." It was Lamont. "We have a rhythm going. It helps us get the job done. It's a real distraction if we have to break someone in."

"I agree with Nick," Selena said. "This isn't Langley. We should leave it alone."

"All of you?" Elizabeth said. "Do I need to remind you that this isn't a democracy?"

"You asked," Nick said. "You really want to disrupt things when someone is loose out there with a bug that could wipe out half the planet?"

Elizabeth looked at her rebellious team. It was the first time she could remember when they'd united against her. She knew Ronnie would back them up. She decided not to push it.

"All right. We'll discuss it in the future."

She picked up her pen and beat a quick tattoo on the desk. "Steph, when do you think you'll have some results?"

"Tonight. I'll check on it when we're finished here."

"Then we're done for now. Be here at nine tomorrow."

Outside, it looked like more snow was coming.

CHAPTER 6

The view from Selena's twelfth floor Washington condo reached across the Potomac to the rolling hills of Virginia and beyond. On a clear day, you could see the Appalachians in the distance. You got a lot of view for the kind of money Selena had paid for it. It never failed to impress Nick each time he saw it. Today everything was obscured by gray haze and snow beginning to fall from a threatening sky.

The remains of breakfast were scattered across the counter. Selena wasn't much of a cook but she could handle bacon and eggs. Nick picked up the plates and rinsed them in the sink before placing them in the stainless steel dishwasher under the counter. He looked at his watch.

"I need to get back to my place and get some fresh clothes before the morning brief," he said.

"If you lived here, you wouldn't have to do that," she said.

"It's a little early in the day for this discussion. It's not like we haven't had it before."

"We have, and it never gets resolved. We're engaged. We sleep together. We work together. Why aren't we living together?"

"Because we both like our own space?"

"You know it's not that simple."

"No, I guess not." He picked up his coffee cup and drained it. "As a matter of fact, I've been thinking about it."

"You have?"

"My apartment is too small, right?"

Selena nodded.

"This place of yours is beautiful," he said, "but it feels like yours, not mine or ours. Just like mine feels like that to you. Why don't we look for a new place, something different we could pick together?"

"A new place? But what about this one?"

"You could sell it. Or keep it as an investment."

She looked at him.

He glanced at his watch again. "I have to go. Think about it." He leaned over and kissed her. "Hey," he said. "It could be fun."

She watched the door close behind him.

It could be fun.

Sure. Why did men seem to think that disrupting everything was fun? She'd finally gotten everything the way she wanted it in the condo. Everything was perfect and now he wanted her to give it up.

Living together had been an issue since the beginning, once they realized they were caught up in something more than an affair. It had taken a lot of ups and downs just to get to this point, where he'd put the ring on her finger. They still hadn't set a date for the wedding. The whole relationship had been like that.

Then there was the issue of her money. She had a lot of it, more than most people would ever see, more than Nick could ever hope to earn or equal. He didn't say much about it, but she knew it was one of the things that came between them. Nick wasn't the kind of person who would let someone else pay his way. This condo alone had cost more than he'd likely make in a lifetime. She'd simply written a check for it to the agent.

Sometimes she wished he'd just let her take care of the money. Then again, if he was a man who was willing to be kept by her, he wouldn't be someone she wanted to keep.

She looked at the clock on the kitchen counter. She needed to take a shower and get dressed and head out to Virginia. She got up and felt a sharp pain in her lower back, right where a bullet had almost left her in a wheelchair for life. Every once in a while her body let her know that she was mortal and getting older. Lately the message had been coming through more often.

You should have taken up something safe, like making documentaries about sharks or jumping off skyscrapers, she thought. *At least sharks don't shoot at you.*

She had to hurry or she'd be late.

CHAPTER 7

General Alexei Ivanovich Vysotsky, Director
of Department S of the *Sluzhba Vneshney Razvedki*,
Russia's Foreign Intelligence Service, sat behind
Lavrenti Beria's old desk and poured himself a glass
of vodka. Vysotsky looked a little bit like Beria,
with piercing black eyes, a broad face and bushy
eyebrows. He was still in his 50s, but years working
in Russian intelligence were beginning to show.
He'd put on weight since his days as a field agent,
adding bulk to his stocky form. His hair had started
to recede and was streaked with silver but Vysotsky
was still handsome enough to draw a woman's eye.
He had the appearance of someone dangerous,
someone who would be a bad man to cross.

It was ten in the morning. This was Alexei's
first drink of the day but it wouldn't be the last.
Vodka for Vysotsky was like water for most people,
though he was starting to notice the effects sooner
and the hangovers were lasting longer.

He finished the drink, thought about another,
and decided against it. The bottle and glass went
back into his desk drawer, right where Beria had
kept his supply when he was chief of the secret
police under Stalin.

Alexei had plenty of reasons for drinking
today. Major Kaminsky had been one of his best
men. He'd been grooming Kaminsky to take the
place of Arkady Korov, killed during a clandestine
operation in America.

Kaminsky had performed at his best, getting
into the North Korean complex and out again with
the samples. A daring and difficult mission with

great risks, accomplished with precision. So how did Kaminsky and his men end up dead while making a simple delivery on Russian territory, safe territory, all the while traveling in a secured, military train?

The whole operation had suddenly turned to shit.

The Kremlin wanted answers. So did Vysotsky. Losing Kaminsky was bad enough. Losing the lethal bacteria the Koreans had developed was worse. Someone had it. The question was who? Who had the resources to stop that train, eliminate the guards and then eliminate Kaminsky and his men? Serious men, *Spetsnaz* soldiers, the best in the world.

A more unsettling question beyond who had done it was why?

Alexei assumed that whoever had stolen the case with the samples knew exactly what was in it. There weren't many who could know that. The Americans, perhaps, but they would never mount an operation like this on Russian soil.

The Chinese almost certainly would know. Beijing's relationship with the Great Leader was erratic, as could only be expected for anyone trying to deal with that lunatic. But the Chinese were his only allies.

They would have known what was hidden in that lab, Vysotsky thought. Still, it would have been difficult for a Chinese hit team to get so far into the interior of the country without being spotted.

Then there was an even more disturbing question. How had the attackers, whoever they were, learned of the transfer to Sverdlovsk? The route, the train, the date and time? It had to be someone within his own organization. There was a traitor somewhere, in Department S or even higher up in SVR. It could even be Russians who had stolen the samples. It was enough to give him a headache.

Alexei sincerely hoped it hadn't been terrorists behind the theft. If the Chechens had done it, it would be a disaster. The possibility had to be considered, but Alexei thought it was a long shot at best. The attack had been too well coordinated, too professional. It had to be a government unit. But who had the balls? The Israelis? The Iranians? For the moment, the Chinese seemed the best bet.

At times like this he missed Korov's practical advice. Arkady had been a good sounding board for his ideas, always practical, fiercely loyal to the *Rodina*, the Motherland. Trustworthy. The best Vysotsky had ever seen in the field. He'd even been able to work with the Americans without becoming infected by their corrupt ideology.

Alexei thought about opening the drawer and reaching again for the vodka but he resisted the urge. He needed a clear head this morning. He was due at the Kremlin in an hour for a meeting with the Security Council. The Director of SVR and his counterpart in the FSB, Russia's internal security service, would be there. The Council reported to the president. The meeting had been called to look into the raid on the train but Alexei knew the real purpose was to assign blame.

At one time the two agencies responsible for Russia's internal and foreign security had been part of the same organization, directorates under the glorious banner of the KGB, back in the day when Alexei had been a young, rising KGB agent. Now they were separate agencies, but the old rivalries and jealousies that had existed during the days of the Soviet Union, the jockeying for position and influence, those things had not changed.

He knew what was expected of him by his boss. It should be relatively easy to lay most of the blame at the feet of the FSB. Even so, Alexei was certain the issue of who had tipped off the raiders was bound to surface.

Somewhere in the Kremlin, knives were being sharpened. It was necessary to find a scapegoat. Alexei Vysotsky was determined that it would not be him. He was going to find out who had those plague samples and get them back.

CHAPTER 8

Rain streaked the facade of a handsome eighteenth century château located a half hour out of Geneva. The building sat on a spit of land jutting into the River Rhône. Water ran in rivulets over a prominent stone bas-relief set over the grand entrance. The carving showed an all-seeing, radiant eye, centered over a nine-pointed star. An inscription bordered the design:

AETERNUS EST ORDUM NOVO

Translated into English, the inscription read:

THE NEW ORDER IS FOREVER

Johannes Gutenberg sat in a dark leather chair in the spacious high-ceilinged library of the château, holding a crystal snifter containing a generous helping of Louis XIII cognac. The polished wooden floor was covered with a fine Persian rug that had once graced the Shah's palace. Rain beat in intermittent gusts against the tall windows of the library, blurring the view of the river flowing by. For a brief instant the sun broke through the dark clouds roiling the afternoon sky and bathed the room in storm light glow.

Gutenberg swirled the smoky amber liquid in his glass and held it to his nose. He inhaled and smiled. There was nothing like it, a distinct aroma that spoke of age and the skill of the master distiller who had created it. It spoke of educated taste, of wealth and power. Wealth and power were two things of great concern to Johannes Gutenberg. Not the getting of them, he had plenty of both. It was the application of them that concerned him, as it had his predecessors in the organization.

AEON had gone through many changes over the centuries. The latest incarnation had emerged during the 1700s but the organization traced its beginning to the time of the Knights Templar. Once it had been part of the Templars but that changed in the thirteenth century when a faction of the order had broken away. Their successors had manipulated the Pope and the King of France to launch the 1307 persecution that shattered the Templars' hold on power. True power lay in the shadows, not on the throne. It was still that way, all these centuries later.

A small group of the original Templars that called themselves the Guardians had escaped the King's soldiers, well aware of who had betrayed them. They still existed and were led by a man Gutenberg knew only as Adam. Their purpose was the defeat and destruction of AEON. It was a hidden war that had been going on for seven hundred years.

The Guardians had never succeeded. If Johannes had his way, they never would. They were troublemakers, all of them. Because of them, plans had been disrupted, important plans. They were the ones who had alerted that American woman's group to AEON's existence.

Gutenberg sipped his cognac. *On the other hand, if it weren't for the Project, I wouldn't be in charge.*

The thought pleased him. Before the Project got involved, there had been nine leaders of AEON, nine wealthy men scattered over the globe. Leadership of the group had always been based on success and the consent of the others. Failure had only one result: death. Interference by the Project in AEON's operations had reduced the leadership board to seven and opened the way for Gutenberg's ascension.

The attrition of leadership could not be allowed to continue and the rules had been changed. Success was still the criterion for remaining as chairman but the death penalty for failure had been rescinded. It made for a more congenial atmosphere. The current board had achieved a good working harmony under Gutenberg.

Success with the Russian operation more than made up for the recent failure in India. The samples of plague stolen by the Russians from the Koreans were safe in Krivi Dass's pharmaceutical laboratories in Zürich. When a vaccine to prevent the disease and a drug to cure it had been found, the next phase of the plan would begin.

Krivi Dass was one of the ruling seven and a close ally of Gutenberg's. Johannes felt comfortable with Krivi. Even his wife liked him. For Gutenberg, that was an important litmus test.

If Johannes had a weak spot, it was for his wife Marta. In Marta's eyes, Johannes was a successful businessman who happened to own one of the oldest banks and greatest fortunes in Europe. Marta saw him as a philanthropist who gave freely to numerous charitable causes, a man with heart. It was doubtful that any of the millions of desperate people who had been pushed further under by Gutenberg's rapacious policies would have agreed with her.

Gutenberg never allowed his feelings for her to interfere with business. Marta would be horrified if she knew what AEON did and what his role was in guiding it. But she would never find out. Johannes was careful to make sure of that.

Johannes Gutenberg was addicted to the use of power, a drug he found more powerful than the finest opium. The application of power brought unfortunate results for some, but that was inevitable when you were building a new world order, where everyone would know their function and place. A world ruled by AEON from behind the scenes. The time was coming when events would make that world possible. Success was closer than it had ever been. Of course there were obstacles that needed to be taken care of before then.

One of those was the Guardians. Johannes sipped his liquor and thought of the trouble they'd caused in the past. The interference of Adam and his group could not be tolerated. It was time to remove them as a factor.

Another problem was Harker's group. That might prove more difficult, but Johannes enjoyed a challenge.

Gutenberg lifted his glass to the rain-swept windows.

To the New Order, he thought, and drank.

CHAPTER 9

It was six in the morning of a freezing February day. Three inches of new snow covered the grounds outside Project headquarters.

Stephanie was early for work, anxious to go over the surveillance report of the North Korean bio weapons facility. The report covered a period of several days before the raid and ended two days later. The computer had compiled a sequence of video shots taken from a hundred and twenty miles up by the NROL-67, the latest in a string of sophisticated spy satellites that formed the U.S. Space and National Reconnaissance Surveillance program.

The videos were astonishing, clear and sharp in every detail. The satellite provided a bird's eye view of everything. Most of the Korean complex was invisible, hidden inside a mountain. A paved road led up to the facility from a broad valley at the foot of the mountain. Anti-aircraft missile batteries were mounted in strategic positions around the complex. The computer identified the missiles as Chinese copies of the Russian V-750, using the obsolete S-75 Dvina launching system. It was the same system that had caused trouble for U.S. pilots over Vietnam. It was an old design but still deadly.

A high fence barred entry to the complex. A guardhouse and gate fronted a wide courtyard and vehicle park. The satellite was programmed to note activity at the compound and capture details of individuals and their movements. Rank designations on sleeves, collars and shoulder boards could be identified. Documents presented for inspection could be read, if the angle was right. Facial features were clear and could be matched by an analyst against a known database of personnel, Korean and otherwise.

Stephanie began watching the videos. She didn't expect to find much before the raid itself but she liked to be thorough. She was looking for anything unusual. Civilian workers left at the end of each day and returned early on the following morning. She noted routine guard changes and the regular arrival on alternate days of a white van. The van would come to the gate, pause for inspection, then be permitted to enter the compound. Two men in white utility uniforms and white caps would get out, unload boxes of produce from the back of the van, and cart them into the unseen tunnel leading into the mountain. Twenty or thirty minutes later they'd reappear with trash, load that into the van and drive off.

Nothing ever seemed to happen at the base except for the civilian traffic, the van delivery and the changing of the guards. She came to the day of the raid. The van pulled up at the usual time. A guard emerged from the hut for the inspection, as he always did. Then everything changed.

It was like watching a movie on television with no sound. A hand holding a pistol came out of the window of the van and fired. The guard stumbled backward and fell. Men in black balaclavas piled out of the van and began shooting at whoever was inside the guard shack. Stephanie saw the windows shatter. One of the men in black was larger than the others. He gestured and the others followed him into the complex.

The dead guard lay sprawled on the courtyard pavement. The van idled in the chill air, wisps of exhaust smoke visible on the video. An Asian looking man in a white uniform stepped out of the cab and lit a cigarette. He had a pistol in one hand.

Exactly twelve minutes and forty-three seconds later, the raiders came out of the compound into the daylight. One of the men carried an aluminum case.

The plague samples, Stephanie thought. The large man she believed to be the leader reached up as if something bothered him under the ski mask and pulled it off to scratch. For a few seconds his face was visible.

Got you, Stephanie thought. She froze the video for a moment and entered commands on her keyboard. The computer began searching the database for a facial recognition match.

He was a white man, not Korean or Chinese or Asian. She restarted the video. The leader got into the back of the van with the others. The driver was already behind the wheel. The truck pulled out through the open gates, past the dead guard, and started down the road. A minute later a thick cloud of smoke and debris billowed out of the entrance to the complex.

Twenty minutes later, the computer signaled a match to the still shot. Stephanie looked at the result and swore under her breath.

Elizabeth won't like this, she thought. She took the printout and went upstairs to Elizabeth's office. Harker was at her desk. It was still early. The others had not yet arrived.

"Good morning," Elizabeth said. She saw Stephanie's expression and the paper in her hand. "What is it."

"I have the results from the satellite surveillance."

"What did you find?"

"It was the Russians who hit the Koreans," Stephanie said. "Zaslon. I identified the leader. He's a Spetsnaz major named Kaminsky. We ID'd him in Aleppo last year."

"The Russians? Damn."

"Yes."

"I never would have expected that. Zaslon is General Vysotsky's group," Elizabeth said. "He had to be under orders from the Kremlin. If the Kremlin's involved, the stakes just got a lot higher. You're sure about the ID?"

"Positive."

"It's an act of war. Why risk war over something like this? The Russians have plenty of nasty stuff of their own. They don't need another bug for their collection."

"Maybe they just want to make sure it can't be used against them."

"That's possible, I guess. It's more likely they want to add it to their biological bag of tricks."

"Why does everyone work so hard at creating things that can kill millions at a time?" Stephanie asked.

"I don't know, Steph. There's something dark in some people, something barbaric and murderous. An impulse that leads to things like this plague being turned into a weapon."

"If I were more religious I'd think it was the work of an evil being. Satanic."

"I think humans can be evil enough," Elizabeth said. "We don't need Satan to explain it. But I admit it would make things easier to understand if it was about a conflict between absolute good and absolute evil."

"A metaphysical war between the forces of darkness and light?"

"Exactly."
"How do you know it isn't?" Stephanie said.

CHAPTER 10

The fact that Johannes Gutenberg loved his wife didn't preclude taking a mistress. After all, it was a traditional way of life for the European rich. It was a man's prerogative if he could afford it and Johannes certainly could. It added status. People saw her with Johannes and envied him. As for Marta, she knew about Valentina and accepted the fact that her husband was unfaithful. She had long ago decided that the practical benefits of being married to Johannes far outweighed the emotional inconvenience of his philandering. Besides, she could take her own lovers if she wished, though lately there had been no one to interest her. As long as she was discrete it wasn't a problem.

Gutenberg wasn't interested in someone who might challenge his sense of entitled superiority. Valentina Rosetti was everything he could desire in a female companion. She had dark black hair that fell to her shoulders in natural curls. High cheekbones and green eyes gave her genuine beauty. She was tall and moved with languid grace. She radiated sexuality and made any man who saw her wonder what she'd be like in bed.

At the moment Valentina lay next to Gutenberg in the bedroom of her apartment in Paris, her long hair spread in a tangle on the pillow. The room smelled of her perfume and the aftermath of sex. Earlier, he'd taken her to dinner and ordered a bottle of 1928 Chateau Gruaud-Larose, a bargain at 1500 euros. Gutenberg enjoyed educating Valentina about the finer things in life. They'd had an excellent meal and a glass of cognac after, then come back to her apartment and made love.

For all her charms, Johannes didn't think much of Valentina's intellectual capability. It was one of the things he liked about her. She was smart enough to present a good impression when they were out together, but she seemed to have no interest in things beyond the gifts and money he gave her. She had no political opinions that he had noticed. She wasn't very interested in world affairs, though he knew she was aware to the minute of upcoming appointments with her masseuse or for a fitting at the salon. She seldom argued with him and never about anything important. And of course she was accomplished in bed. In short, she was everything a man could want in a mistress. Sometimes Johannes blessed his lucky stars when he thought of her. She was almost too good to be true.

She was.

Valentina's real name wasn't Rossi, it was Antipov. She'd been born in St. Petersburg, not Italy as Johannes believed. She'd never known her father. Her mother had been killed in a meaningless car accident three years before.

Valentina's mother had been a decorated KGB agent during the old Soviet regime, trusted enough to be sent abroad to America and the other western nations. Quick intelligence and natural athletic ability, coupled with her mother's stellar record as a loyal servant of the state, made Valentina a natural for selection as a future agent. She'd been brought up under the watchful guidance of her mother's minders, groomed from an early age as an *agent provocateur*.

Like her mother before her, Valentina was a spy.

Valentina worked for Alexei Vysotsky, part of a small group of experienced SVR agents Vysotsky ran separately from the rest of his organization. She cared not at all for Gutenberg but found it easy to enjoy the decadent comforts he provided. He was not a particularly skilled or demanding lover and their liaisons were infrequent enough that she didn't consider it a burden. Valentina was a consummate actress. Her cries of passion in bed would have convinced any man that he was a match for Casanova.

Vysotsky had explained to Valentina why Gutenberg was important. The Swiss banker was the driving force behind an effort to derail the new financial alliance between Brazil, Russia, India and China. BRICS intended to establish a new base currency to replace the dollar as the world's standard. If the alliance succeeded, the U.S. would no longer be able to dominate world commerce as it had in the past. If the alliance fell apart, years of careful planning and difficult political negotiations with Russia's strange bedfellows would be wasted. The United States would remain dominant. A potential war with China would become more likely.

As usual after one of their bouts in bed, Johannes lay back with a cigarette and a glass of cognac. Valentina reached over and laid her arm across his chest, pressing up against him with her breasts. She knew he liked that. At times like this Johannes was relaxed, his guard down. He liked to boast about his business deals, secure in the knowledge that his mistress understood nothing at all of what he was talking about. More than one of these pillow conversations had found their way to Vysotsky's desk.

"It's been too long since I saw you," she said. "I've been lonely."

"Don't pout, darling. You know I have affairs to attend to. It's been a very good week for me. I managed to create real difficulties for people who were opposing my plans."

"What people?" She snuggled closer to him.

"Russians, my dear, men who have no understanding of the world. All they understand is force. They lack the devious political subtlety of our western sophistication."

What an arrogant bastard, Valentina thought. *Russians were applying devious political sophistication before Machiavelli was a gleam in his father's eye.*

She looked at him wide-eyed, as if amazed at his skill in manipulating his enemies.

"What did you do?"

"The details are unimportant. They had something I wanted. They thought it was secure, but I took it from them. Now I'll be able to use it against them, when the time is right."

The General will want to know about this, she thought.

"What was it?"

She felt him tense against her. "It doesn't matter. Don't bother yourself about it."

Change the subject. "I saw a nice bracelet today on the Champs-Élysées. Do you think we could go look at it tomorrow?"

His body relaxed. "Of course. And perhaps pay a visit to that salon you like. The one with a designer who knows how to fit you."

"Ooh, Johannes. Thank you."

Later, after they'd made love again and Gutenberg was asleep, Valentina thought about

what she would report to Vysotsky. She didn't know
what it was that Gutenberg had stolen but the
general would, she was sure.

CHAPTER 11

Nick left his apartment and took the elevator down to the first floor. Things were quiet. Unless the pager on his belt brought him to Virginia, the team had a rare day off. He was meeting Selena for breakfast and after that, they had an appointment with a real estate agent. Nick was looking forward to the morning. Things were going really well between them. Selena had come around to the idea of a new place and now she was enthusiastic about it.

He stepped out of his building and felt the cold bite into him. A black Cadillac limo idled by the curb. There was only one Cadillac that ever waited for Nick.

Adam, Nick thought. *It has to mean trouble. What now?*

The driver held the passenger door open for him. Nick got in the back. The driver closed the door.

The Cadillac had been modified with a thick panel of opaque, black glass that split the rear into two separate compartments. The driver was out of sight behind a similar panel in the front. Nick's door window was blacked out and impossible to see through.

Nick had never seen Adam's face and had no idea who he was. He'd never heard his voice, except through the distortion of electronic masking. For all he knew, Adam could be a woman. A speaker allowed for communication between the two sides of the rear compartment. A drawer could be opened in the glass if something needed to be passed from one side to the other.

Aside from Adam's modifications, Cadillac had designed the Presidential model for people with a serious need for security. The turbocharged diesel engine produced over 500 horsepower. The car had five inch thick armor plate. Nothing less than a .50 caliber round could trouble the bullet proof glass. Run flat tires with steel sidewalls and special compounds would keep rolling long after they'd been shot and punctured. The engine compartment, the underside of the car and the trunk were all armored. The Cadillac was a luxury tank.

"Hello, Nick."

Adam's electronic voice sounded in the speaker by Nick's ear. There was something in the speech pattern that made Nick think Adam was an older man.

"Adam."

The heavy car began to roll silently through the streets of Washington.

"Please look in the compartment on the side of your door," Adam said.

Nick reached into the compartment and took out a sealed envelope.

"That envelope contains a phone number you can use to reach me in case of an emergency."

Adam had never given Nick a way to contact him before. "You anticipate trouble?"

"I always anticipate trouble. Especially now. AEON is planning a terrible adventure."

"I thought they were finished after the last time."

"Your efforts set them back but they've recovered."

"What are they doing now?"

"Are you familiar with the Bible?"

The question seemed to come out of the blue. "What do you mean? If you want to know if I can quote chapter and verse, no."

"How about the Book of Revelations? The Four Horsemen?"

I don't like where this is headed, Nick thought.

The heavy car slowed, then picked up speed. The electronic voice echoed from the speaker.

"The Four Horsemen are Conquest, War, Famine and Pestilence, in that order." AEON has decided to shift things around a little."

Nick shivered, for no good reason. "What do you mean?"

"You know about the plague the North Koreans were working on."

It was a statement, not a question.

"Yes."

"A Spetsnaz unit from Vysotsky's Zaslon group raided the Korean lab and took the plague samples."

"The Russians? But what's that got to do with AEON?"

"AEON took it from them in turn. They intend to target specific countries and release it."

"What? Why? What advantage is there in that?"

"A plague epidemic would create chaos and confusion. In the target countries, it would disrupt everything. Government services, transport and food supplies, infrastructure maintenance, anything and everything where people have to work together to accomplish something. There would be massive quarantines, internment camps, martial law. The economy of a target nation would collapse. That's one goal."

"They have more than one?"

"AEON wants to establish a world where those who are considered less desirable will be eliminated or used as labor. They believe there are too many people in the world. They want to reduce the world population."

Nick let the words sink in. "You're saying they want a population die-off and are going to use this disease to make it happen?" His voice echoed with doubt. "That's hard to believe."

"You're having trouble believing it because an idea like that doesn't fit with who you are," Adam said. "A decent person can't really grasp the idea that someone would plan the deaths of hundreds of millions."

"Who do they plan to go after?" Nick asked.

"China, for one. That's what the Indian misadventure you were involved in was about. If that missile had gotten through, it would have destroyed most of their central banking system. Brazil, Russia and India are also on their list. Africa is a potential target. There are vast resources there, inconveniently tied up by governments that won't cooperate in being plundered."

The car halted briefly. Nick wondered where he was. Nothing could be seen through the opaque glass. For all he knew, they were just driving around the block.

Adam continued. "AEON's leader is a banker named Johannes Gutenberg. The four countries I mentioned have been working on creating a new currency standard to challenge the dollar's supremacy. China has already established the Asian Industrial Bank to compete with the IMF and the World Bank. If they succeed, Gutenberg and the others in AEON will lose billions. He can't allow that to happen. China is the primary target. If he brings down Beijing, the BRICS alliance will fall apart. The plague is a means to an end. Gutenberg doesn't care if millions die in the process."

"That's evil," Nick said.

"Yes, it is."

"What's to keep them from getting sick themselves, once they let this stuff loose?" Nick asked. "Our understanding is that there's no cure."

"They're looking for ways to cure and prevent it," Adam said. "They haven't got it yet but my information is that they're close to a breakthrough on a vaccine. When they have something that works, they'll release the plague."

"What are you asking me to do?"

"Your group has to destroy the labs and samples before they can release it. The labs are in Switzerland and India, part of the Dass pharmaceutical complex. There are a lot of separate facilities. I don't know which ones have the samples."

"Dass. Krivi Dass?" Nick said. "He was part of that attempt to launch a missile at China. We couldn't prove his involvement."

"That's him," Adam said. "He's part of AEON's leadership."

The car stopped, started up again. The ride was quiet, comfortable. It was a strange conversation, surreal. He was riding in total luxury and talking about madmen who wanted to unleash death upon the world.

"I don't think there's much time to stop this," Adam said. "There's something else."

The drawer between the two sides of the rear compartment slid open. Inside was a gold coin.

"Please take the coin, Nick."

Nick picked it up. It felt heavy in his hand. The coin was a little larger than a quarter. One side bore the image of two knights riding a single horse. The other side depicted a domelike structure with a cross imposed upon it.

The seal of the Knights Templar.

The drawer closed and Adam's electronic voice came through the speaker. "If anyone approaches you in the future and gives you one of these coins, you will know they come from my organization."

The car came to a stop. Nick's door clicked open.

"Good hunting, Nick. I'll be in touch."

Nick got out and found himself back in front of his building. He watched Adam's limo ease out into the street. From somewhere in the heavy traffic, a powerful red motorcycle with two riders wearing black leathers and helmets with smoked face shields came up fast behind the Cadillac. The passenger tossed a dark object onto the roof. It stuck to the top of the car with a metallic clang. The bike accelerated away.

Nick opened his mouth to shout a warning when an explosion ripped the car apart and knocked him to the sidewalk. Windows shattered all along the street.

The burning, twisted remains of Adam's armored car drifted to the curb and stopped. Nick got to his feet and looked at the wreckage. There was no chance anyone inside the car had survived.

I could have been riding in that.

He took out his phone and called Harker.

CHAPTER 12

Harker brought the team in for an emergency meeting.

Ronnie was back and looked a lot better than the last time Nick had seen him. Ronnie was Navajo and he'd gone home to be healed in the old ways, after wounds he'd taken in the Philippines almost killed him. His uncle was a Navajo singer, one of a few left who still knew the healing songs and ceremonies that formed the traditional heart of Navajo culture.

"Man, am I glad to see your ugly face," Nick said. "How are you feeling?"

"Good."

Ronnie was broad, stocky and muscular, with the kind of classic features seen in pictures of the Old West. He looked like he belonged on the back of a horse with a lever action Winchester in his hand and war paint on his face.

"I don't know what you did but it worked," Nick said.

"A sweat. Some singing, that's all. We have a ceremony for just about everything."

"Well, I'm glad you're back." Nick didn't push him for details. He figured Ronnie would tell him about it or he wouldn't. The healing ceremonies were sacred in Navajo tradition, private.

They went into Harker's office. It wasn't often Ronnie got embarrassed or ill at ease but when Selena and Stephanie hugged him, he managed it. Lamont just shook his hand.

"Welcome back, Ronnie," Elizabeth said.

"Thanks, Director." They all sat down.

"You ready for the field again?" she said.

"Yeah, I'm ready."

"All right, then. We have a lot to talk about. First, it was the Russians who took the plague samples."

"The Russians?" Selena said. "Who?"

"General Vysotsky's group."

The Russians, Selena thought. *The ones who killed my father.*

"It turns out that the Russians are only part of the problem." Elizabeth turned to Nick. "Tell them about Adam."

No one had ever met Adam except Nick, but they all knew about him. It was Adam who'd first warned them about AEON. Nick repeated what Adam had told him and described the attack on the car. When he finished, there was silence in the room.

"These guys never quit, do they?" Lamont said.

"If it wasn't them it would be someone else," Elizabeth said.

"Adam said the leader is a banker named Gutenberg," Nick said. "That's a place to start."

"Does he have a first name?" Stephanie asked.

"Johannes."

Stephanie entered the name on her laptop keyboard, linked to the enormous power of the Crays downstairs. The response was instant. A picture came up on the wall monitor. Gutenberg looked like what he was, a Swiss banker. He wore designer glasses with thin black rims. His face was unsmiling in the photograph, his lips pulled primly together. He was wearing an expensive suit and perfectly knotted tie. He looked to be about sixty years old. His eyes were watery green, cold and indifferent.

"Johannes Gutenberg," she said. "Owns and operates an old line European bank based in Geneva. He lives in an eighteenth century château that's a favorite in the picture postcard industry, right on the Rhône."

"Big bucks," Lamont said.

"The biggest. Gutenberg is listed in the top 50 richest men in the world." Her fingers flew over the keys. "His bank has investments in everything from agriculture to arms manufacture."

"Pharmaceuticals? Bio research?" Nick asked.

"Those too." She entered another command. "Through his bank he owns shell corporations and companies all over the world. He's everywhere. He's protected by Swiss banking laws from most of the regulatory issues of other governments. His personal fortune is stashed in Andorra, where it can't be touched."

"Where's Andorra?" Lamont asked. "I never heard of it."

"It's in the Eastern Pyrenees, bordered by Spain and France," Elizabeth said.

"I went skiing there once," Selena said. "It's tiny, a principality. It's famous for being a tax haven. If you want to hide money or avoid taxes, it's a good bet. But you need quite a bit of money to open accounts there. It's old Europe, a remnant from the days of princes and kings. The scenery is beautiful and it's very popular with tourists."

"What about Krivi?" Nick asked. "Adam said he's part of AEON's leadership, along with Gutenberg. What can you find out about him?"

Stephanie entered another search. "Krivi Dass. He's almost as wealthy as Gutenberg. Runs Dass Pharmaceuticals, which is huge. Krivi is one of the big boys in drugs. He has research labs and manufacturing facilities in Zürich and Mumbai."

"Adam thought the plague samples were in one of those labs," Nick said. "We need to find and destroy them."

"That's easier said than done," Elizabeth said. "We don't know where they are. They could be in Switzerland or India."

"Then that's the next step, get into the labs and look for them. We could start in Switzerland. That's Gutenberg's home base. If we don't find anything there, the samples will be in India."

"We can't just go barging in. The Swiss are touchy about things like that. It would create a huge problem for the president if you got caught. He's not going to authorize it without hard evidence."

"He doesn't have to know about it," Nick said. "How many times has he turned a blind eye to what we do? Isn't this what he pays us for?"

"Adam never steered us wrong in the past," Selena said. "If AEON killed him, they're getting ready to act."

Nick said, "Adam didn't think there was much time left before they let the plague loose. Director, send us in. We have to recover those samples."

"I can pin down the lab locations," Stephanie said.

They waited in silence while Elizabeth made up her mind. "All right," she said. "If we have a reasonable certainty of the location, you go in. Just don't get caught."

CHAPTER 13

Krivi Dass' office took up half of the top floor of Dass Pharmaceuticals' Zürich headquarters. The room featured a wall of windows overlooking the old city and the sprawling rail yards of the Zürich train station at the junction of the Sihl and Limmat Rivers. Beyond, Lake Zürich was a shimmering mirror of blue under the winter sky. The snow-capped Swiss Alps stretched across the horizon in the distance. It was an amazing view. For all its beauty, Krivi sometimes wished it was of his native city of Mumbai and its jumbled chaos and dirt and disorder, as different from the obsessively clean streets of Switzerland could be.

Krivi was in his mid-seventies, a thin man, tall for an Indian. His skin was a medium dark brown. He wore a light brown suit of exquisite material, a dark silk tie and polished brown shoes. Gold cufflinks peeked out from the sleeves of a Turnbull and Asher shirt that was whiter than the snow on the distant Alpine peaks. His eyes were dark and impenetrable. He had taken to wearing prescription glasses with tinted lenses and round gold frames. He thought they leant a distinguished look, rather like a professor or doctor. In truth, the glasses made him look like a malevolent Ghandhi.

Sitting across from Krivi was Karl Schmidt, his chief research scientist. Schmidt had classic Nordic looks, blue eyes and close-cropped blond hair. With his athletic build and broad chest, he looked like he'd stepped from an Olympic poster advertising the German games of 1936.

Schmidt was old enough to head up Krivi's extensive research program but he was too young to remember the SS laboratories overseen by his grandfather in Germany during the Hitler years. After the war, his grandfather and then his father had worked for the Soviets in East Germany, looking for ways to make trouble for the West. If Schmidt's grandfather had still been alive, he would have been amazed at the technology and equipment Karl had at his disposal for research into the diseases that existed to savage the human body. And if he had still been alive, he would have been proud of the way in which his grandson was carrying on the family scientific tradition.

Human subjects were not as easily persuaded to participate in experiments as in the days when his grandfather pursued Himmler's medical "research." Even so, there were always volunteers willing to risk their lives for the generous compensation and free medical care Schmidt offered. It always amazed him that people would willingly expose themselves to life threatening disease, but human nature was anything but rational. Greed or desperation often clouded people's better judgement. It wasn't his problem, after all.

Up until now, participation in the tests had been a bad bet for the subject.

"Well?" Krivi said. "Is there any progress?"

"Yes and no," Schmidt said. "The latest vaccine shows promise but I still haven't found a drug to cure the disease. It defeats everything I throw at it. The Koreans managed to make the bacteria more virulent and at the same time more resistant. I can slow it down and keep the septicemia at bay for a day or two but then it comes back stronger than before. Death follows within a day, two at the most. It's rather unpleasant."

"Have there been any issues with the subjects?"

"None. We choose only those with no families or relations we can locate. We are well protected, legally. They all thought they knew what they were getting into and signed the appropriate documents. One of the advantages of working here is the Swiss legal system and body of law. It's a thing of beauty, rock solid and binding. Their deaths would be seen as an unfortunate result of a gamble that didn't pay off for them. But no one will ever know about them."

"Good. What is your projection on the vaccine?"

"I really am encouraged by the latest results. We've advanced from primates to human subjects. There are three, two men and a woman, who were infected four days ago. So far they show no symptoms. It's too early to know if the vaccine will be effective in the long run, but I'm optimistic. If they're symptom free in a week, we'll be ready for the next phase."

"Tell me about the disease."

"Ah," Schmidt said, "the disease. It's not a good thing to contract, let me tell you."

"What are the symptoms?"

"Fever begins within two days of exposure, combined with nasal drainage that causes sneezing and coughing. The lungs begin to fill with fluid. At that point the subject becomes highly infectious to anyone coming near. The fever becomes quite high and is followed by diarrhea and vomiting, much like a viral infection. The progression from exposure to death takes about ten days. "

"Fatality rate?"

"It's always fatal," Schmidt said.

"One hundred percent?"

Schmidt nodded. "The septicemia appears on the fourth day and the fingers and toes become necrotic. Black blotches appear, usually on the torso. One of my lab workers said they look like flowers. It gave me an idea for a codename for the disease. I call it black rose."

"How very poetic," Krivi said. "Plague is bacterial. Why haven't you been able to kill it with antibiotics?"

"It's really very clever, what the Koreans did," Schmidt said, "even brilliant. They used genetic manipulation on samples of the plague recreated from the genomes of plague victims. The result is something that's never been seen before. Every time we hit it with something new, it mutates into a resistant form. So far we've found nothing that will kill it once the subject is infected. But I believe we have a vaccine that works to prevent infection."

"Good," Krivi said.

"It would help to have a larger test population."

Krivi brushed a tiny speck of lint from the sleeve of his brown suit. "Perhaps it's time to initiate a wider trial."

"I've been thinking about that," Schmidt said. "There is a free health clinic operating in Brazil as part of our Corporate PR campaign. It's perfect for our purpose. We could infect some subjects and inoculate others with the vaccine at the same time. No one would suspect anything. It would be put down to natural causes if there was an outbreak and it would provide an excellent field test. But without the cure, it could get out of control."

"Is the test site isolated?"

"Yes. It's a small village on the border of an Indian reservation in the far north of the country. It could be quarantined."

Krivi thought about it. "Go ahead and begin."

"Yes, sir."

"Good work, Karl. Keep me updated."

After Schmidt was gone, Krivi swiveled his chair and looked out toward the mountains. A sudden twinge in his chest made him wince. The twinges were coming more frequently, these last few months. Odd pains, hints of mortality.

It had been years since Krivi had given any serious thought about what might or might not await him in the afterlife. For one thing, he wasn't at all sure there was an afterlife and if there was, he had nothing to say about it. He'd been raised in a culture steeped in the concept of karma and rebirth and endless reverberations of the actions one took in one's lifetime. Krivi had decided long ago that since he couldn't possibly anticipate all the consequences of his actions, he might as well not worry about them.

Since the day he'd come to that realization, he'd never looked back. All that mattered was the game of wealth and power, the heady addiction of control over the destiny of millions. With the others in AEON he was about to claim power that would make any of the great conquerors of history envious.

The phone on his desk rang, with a peculiar, old-world sound that had vanished from modern instruments. This particular phone had once graced the study of Nicholas II, the last Czar of Russia. Krivi enjoyed using the antique. It seemed fitting.

"Yes."

"Krivi, my friend. How are you?"

The phone was old, but the quality of voice was quite good. Gutenberg's voice was clear and sharp.

"Well, Johannes. And you?"

"Excellent, especially today. One of the obstacles to our success has been removed."

"Oh?"

"We will no longer be troubled by the annoying Adam."

"That's good news. Tell me what happened," Krivi said.

"He had a car accident," Gutenberg said. "I had hoped to eliminate one of the Project people also, but the timing didn't quite work out. It doesn't matter, there's plenty of time to take care of them."

"You're certain Adam is out of the way?"

"Oh, yes, there's no way he could have survived. His organization will be in disarray. Tell me, how are you progressing? Will we be ready soon?"

"We're about to begin field testing." Krivi told him about Brazil. "The test will give us good data on how fast the disease spreads in a human population and the effectiveness of the vaccine. After that, the only thing is to find the right combination of drugs to combat it."

"As long as the vaccine works and can be produced in enough quantity to protect our personnel, a cure is not essential at this point."

"Schmidt seems confident it will work," Krivi said.

"Herr Schmidt is one of our greatest assets. We are lucky to have him."

"Have you decided on the initial target for wider dispersal yet?"

"I'm leaning toward Brazil. Now that the Russians are busy wrecking their own economy, eliminating Brazil might be enough to accomplish our goal."

"There's still China to deal with. And New Delhi."

"Yes. Well. Let's see what happens in Brazil. If successful, we'll move on to China. Depending on results there, we'll let Beijing know it could easily happen to them."

"They might not believe it."

"That would be a mistake," Gutenberg said.

CHAPTER 14

The team gathered in Harker's office. It was Sunday. Days off were no longer on the schedule.

"What have you found, Steph?" Elizabeth said.

"Krivi has biohazard labs in Zürich and Mumbai. I can't say with certainty which one we should target."

"We could go after the guy who runs things," Ronnie said. "What's his name, Gutenberg. Grab him and make him tell us where those samples are."

"We can't, not yet," Elizabeth said. "Same with Krivi."

"The Koreans didn't have a vaccine or a cure, is that right?" Selena asked.

"That's right."

"Then Krivi must have a team of people working on it. Whatever AEON has in mind for that bug, they'll want to protect themselves. Who's Krivi's best medical researcher? Maybe we could find out where the samples are by watching him. See where he goes to work in the morning."

Elizabeth looked at her. "That's so simple, it's brilliant. I should have thought of that."

"It should be easy to find out who it is," Stephanie said.

She tapped on the keyboard of the laptop she always seemed to have with her.

"Krivi's company has a corporate website with all the typical blurbs. It's got photos of top personnel."

They waited. Stephanie entered a command and the monitor on the wall lit with a picture of a blond man in a white lab coat. He was smiling for the camera but the smile failed to reach his eyes.

"Guy looks like he needs a fancy black uniform and a few flags," Lamont said.

"He does have that look, doesn't he," Stephanie said. "This is Karl Schmidt, the chief research scientist for Krivi's company. He's got quite a list of credentials. The man's a genius. He'd be the one Krivi would use."

"Where does he live?" Nick asked.

"It doesn't say. It does say that the main research lab is in Zürich. I imagine he lives there."

"I like Selena's idea," Nick said. "We find out where he lives, go to Zürich, stake out his house and see where he goes. He has to be working on the samples."

"Then what?" Elizabeth asked.

"If we think we know where they've got the samples, we break in and steal them back."

"That's not a good idea," Selena said.

"Why not?"

"If this thing is as bad as it's made out to be, we can't handle it. What are we going to do, put on hazmat suits and raid the facility? Put the samples in a baggie?"

"I hadn't thought about it. We'll think of something."

"We don't have to steal the samples," Ronnie said. "We just have to destroy them, along with the research. It's probably in the same building."

"Typical Jarhead thinking," Lamont said. "When in doubt, blow it up."

"So?" Ronnie said. "Your point?"

"Seems like a good idea to me," Nick said.

"Hold on," Elizabeth said. "You can't just blow up a Swiss research lab."

"Why not?" Nick asked.

"Well, because you can't. It's Swiss. They're neutral."

"They may be, but Krivi isn't," Nick said. "We can't take the samples with us. We can't leave them behind. What else are we going to do?"

"He's right, Director," Selena said. "We have to destroy it."

Elizabeth looked at her pen and forced herself not to pick it up.

"I hope I don't regret this," she said. "Steph, find out where Schmidt lives. Nick, you'd better make damn sure you've picked the right building before you push the button. Take the Gulfstream and leave tomorrow."

"What about weapons? We need more than pistols for this in case we run into opposition. MP5s, C-4, detonators. Not so easy to take those through Swiss customs."

"Take them on the plane. You'll have diplomatic passports, they won't search you."

"While you're arranging things, how about a safe house? We could be there a while."

"I'll see what I can do."

"I always wanted to see Switzerland in the winter," Lamont said.

"Lots of snow," Ronnie said. "And mountains."

"Do you ski, Nick?" Selena asked.

CHAPTER 15

Zürich in winter was everything the tourist magazines said it was, a picture-perfect example of old world Europe. Six inches of fresh snow lay over everything, turning the city into a calendar shot for the travel agents.

The safe house was a five story building in the *Aussersihl*, a district of residential buildings and shops lying between the Sihl river and the train station. Lamont sat down on a low couch and surveyed the room.

"Beats the place we got in India," he said.

"Harker borrowed it from Langley."

"I wonder if she sees Hood outside of work," Lamont said.

"Like a couple, you mean?"

"Why not?"

Nick shook his head. "I can't picture that."

"What's the plan?" Ronnie asked.

"Pick rooms and get settled in. Check the gear and contact Harker. See if there's anything to eat in the kitchen."

"We passed a market on the corner," Selena said.

"I want to stay in as much as possible. The locals might assume we're tourists but we stand out. No need to call more attention to ourselves than we have to. Selena, you speak the language. If we need something, you'll have to get it."

"No problem. I can pass for German, they won't think anything of that."

"I'll set up the comm," Lamont said.

"Let's unpack the weapons," Nick said.

They had four MP-5s with thirty round clips and extra ammo for each. There were eight kilos of C-4, enough to take out a fair sized target.

They had vests that would stop most pistol rounds, though a .45 would knock the wearer down. The vests weren't always proof against a Kalashnikov or FN but they were a lot better than nothing. They were uncomfortable and heavy. If things worked as they should, they wouldn't need them. But things didn't always go as planned. When it was time to go in, they'd wear the vests.

Lamont activated the comm link and brought Stephanie on line. Her image was clear on the screen of their laptop.

"I've located Schmidt," she said. "He lives in an exclusive apartment building in the north central part of the city, north of the lake. Krivi has a villa on the eastern side. Very upscale."

"Have you figured out where Schmidt works?" Nick asked.

"No. I haven't spotted him. A lot of people go in and out of his building and the satellite isn't always in position. You're going to have to put eyes on him. There's a garage in his building where he keeps his car. The registration says it's a red BMW 635, a classic. The number is ZH 478664."

"Okay."

"I'm sending you the locations of the laboratories. It's possible the samples are in a lab on the second floor of Krivi's corporate headquarters, but I'm leaning toward another location, just outside the city. That makes more sense to me. It's out of town, private, and there's plenty of room for a bio-containment set up. I'm sending a picture and the architectural plans."

The plans and address scrolled out of a printer Lamont had set up on the dining table next to the open laptop.

"That's great work, Steph."

"It was easy. The plans are a matter of public record. The picture comes from the corporate website. I think it's probably the best bet, but you need to confirm it."

"If Schmidt goes there tomorrow, we'll check it out after everyone's gone home."

"Anything else?"

"No."

"Good hunting," Stephanie said. She broke the connection.

CHAPTER 16

Ronnie sat next to Nick in the front seat of their rented Range Rover, parked down the street from Schmidt's apartment building. Selena and Lamont were in a second car on the other side of the city, staked out where they could watch the entrance to Krivi's sprawling home. It was still early and very cold. Nick kept the heater and defroster on. He wasn't worried about being spotted. A car idling in the frosty Swiss morning wouldn't attract attention. Schmidt had no reason to suspect anyone was watching him.

A red BMW emerged from the underground garage of the building and turned into traffic. Ronnie eyed the plate through binoculars.

"That's him," Ronnie said.

Nick put the Range Rover in gear and pulled in behind Schmidt, half a block behind. Traffic signs were everywhere, large blue signs with white letters and arrows and unpronounceable names. Nick didn't try to memorize the route. For one thing, he didn't know where Schmidt was going. For another, the GPS unit on the Range Rover's dash would record everything. If they needed to retrace it later, it wouldn't be a problem.

After twenty minutes, the traffic began to thin. They were heading west, out of the city. Nick dropped back but kept Schmidt in sight.

He touched the transceiver in his ear. "Selena, you copy?"

"Copy, Nick."

"We're on Schmidt. It looks like he's headed for the lab outside the city. What's happening on your end?"

"Krivi came out about five minutes ago and got into a chauffeured Mercedes. We're four cars behind him. He's going west, but we don't know where, yet. Could be his corporate building or maybe the lab."

"Stay on him and let me know if he's coming this way. Krivi is AEON and it's possible he might recognize one of us. Be careful he doesn't spot you."

"Copy that."

"Out."

"Krivi?" Ronnie said.

"On the road to somewhere. They're behind him."

Ahead, the red BMW slowed and turned into a sloping drive leading to a low, sand-colored building. It was three stories high, landscaped with low shrubs and flowerbeds buried under snow. The building had black tinted windows. A separate wing at the end had no windows at all. A tall chimney rose above it. Nick slowed as they drove past the entrance.

Gold letters inset into stone on either side of the drive announced Dass Pharmaceuticals. The drive was barred by an iron gate set into a low wall along the front of the property. A guardhouse stood to the side. Schmidt's car stopped and a guard emerged into the cold, his breath making small clouds as he bent over and looked into the car. He was dressed in a dark blue paramilitary uniform with a military style cap. He had an MP-5 slung over his shoulder and a pistol on his hip. A second man watched from within the guardhouse.

The guard stepped back and saluted. The gate opened and Schmidt drove through.

"Pretty serious firepower for a security guard," Ronnie said. "Backup, too. I wonder what they've got in there."

"Plague samples, maybe," Nick said. "Krivi must have serious clout to get permission for weapons like that."

"Hey, it's Switzerland, the land of happy cows, Swiss cheese and banks," Ronnie said. "Money always talks."

"That wall doesn't put up much of a barrier. I'll bet he's got a hell of an alarm system. Motion sensors, laser beams, the works."

"I can get past those. I brought along a few gadgets Harker got from Langley's dirty tricks shop."

"Now we know where Schmidt works," Nick said. "Ten to one those samples are stashed somewhere inside."

"Yeah. Could be anywhere inside, though," Ronnie said. "That's a lot of floor space."

"We'll find it."

Nick drove on until he came to a place where he could turn around and park on the side of the road. His earpiece sounded.

"Nick, you copy?"

"Copy."

"Krivi is headed your way," Selena said. "He should get there in about five minutes."

"We're about a mile on the other side of the lab. Meet us there. Eyeball the layout as you go by."

"Got it. Out."

Twelve minutes later, Lamont and Selena pulled up behind them. Selena got out and came over. Nick rolled down his window.

"Krivi went into the building," Selena said. ""What now?"

"Now we go back to the safe house and make a plan. Did you get a good look as you went by?"

"Yes. It looks too easy. There must be hidden alarms."

"I had the same thought. You saw the weapons?"

"I did. I wonder if those guards are here around the clock?"

"We'll find out tonight," Nick said.

CHAPTER 17

Alexei Vysotsky finished reading the report from Valentina Antipov, AKA Valentina Rosetti, and felt the tightness around his forehead that meant his blood pressure was going up. He took a deep breath and reached for the bottle of *Moskovskaya* vodka he kept in his desk drawer.

Gutenberg, he thought. *You son of a whore.*

Valentina's report didn't identify what it was that Gutenberg had stolen from the "Russians" but Vysotsky was convinced it was the sample case taken from the dead hands of Major Kaminsky. What else could it be? Alexei had to admit it had taken real balls to snatch the case on Russian soil from under the watchful eyes of a Spetsnaz squad. It meant that he'd better not make the mistake of underestimating Gutenberg as an enemy.

Alexei was under a lot of pressure to find whoever was responsible for the raid on the train. It didn't help that he was convinced someone in his own organization, someone high up, had told Gutenberg where and when the samples were being transferred. But who? Who had the knowledge? It was a very short list.

The Director of SVR, Boris Vishinski. His deputy, Vladamir Kamarov. The Interior Minister and probably the president. Possibly an aide, someone in Kamarov's or Vishinski's office who had seen the memo about the transfer. Major Kaminsky himself. If Kaminsky was the traitor he had already paid for his treachery, but Alexei didn't believe it was him. The only other person who knew was himself.

If he couldn't prove it was someone else, he'd end up getting the blame. The Soviet Union was gone but the old ways of dealing with difficult internal problems were returning. In this case, blame could mean a bullet in the back of his head.

Vysotsky hoped it was an aide who was the traitor, but in his heart he knew it was one of his two bosses, Kamarov or Vishinski. It would be an unpopular accusation. He needed solid proof and he needed it soon, before the finger pointed at him.

He poured a water glass full of vodka and downed half of it and felt some of the tension leave his body. He always thought better after a drink or two. One of the reasons he'd reached his present high position within the ranks of SVR was his ability to drink and stay focused when the vodka was flowing. Others became careless, they made mistakes. Not Vysotsky.

Vysotsky considered why someone would betray his country. The usual reasons were depressingly common. Money. A woman. Anger at a slight or failure to gain recognition or promotion. Belief in another's ideology. Misguided idealism. A sense of secret power.

All of those were good reasons, if any reason for treachery was a good one. But which of those, if any, applied to his two chief suspects? Alexei took out a pad and began making a list.

Power.
Failure/anger @ system/individuals.
A woman.
Ideology/belief/idealism.
Money.

Both men had power, public and secret, and plenty of it. There was only so much power to be had and they had both gone about as far as they would. Kamarov could become Director of SVR in the event Vishinski stepped down or was removed, but that was the extent of it and was uncertain at best. Power couldn't be ruled out as a motive, but how did the theft of the plague samples further that aim? It wasn't immediately apparent. Vysotsky put a question mark next to power.

Neither man had any reason to feel slighted by the system. They had succeeded where many had failed. It was likely there was a personal grudge or two in their histories but enough of a grudge to betray the nation that had rewarded them? Vysotsky didn't think so. He drew a line through failure.

Kamarov was widowed and was not involved with anyone, as far as Alexei knew. Men like Kamarov and Vishinski were routinely surveilled. If Kamarov was seeing someone, it would have been discovered. Vishinski was married, well satisfied with a vetted mistress on the side that he kept in an elegant apartment in Moscow. Alexei crossed a woman off his list as a possible motive.

Neither man had shown the least deviation in political correctness, but such things could be kept hidden. Who knew what a man really thought? Both men were hard liners, like Alexei himself. He knew both men well and he didn't think either one would be tempted by the illusions of the West. It was unlikely, a real stretch. Vysotsky crossed off idealism as a possibility. These were not idealistic men.

That left money. Neither man had any particular problems with money. Kamarov's uncle was one of the hated oligarchs and his favorite nephew lacked for nothing. Vishinski was well off by Russian standards, even by western ones. Their positions entitled them to many perks and benefits.

Even so, Vysotsky thought, *for some there is never enough..*

He decided to dig into the finances of the two men. He'd have to be careful. If they discovered what he was doing, the hammer would fall. It was the nature of life in the circles of Russian power. It had always been that way, since the days of the czars.

Alexei drained the rest of the vodka. Then he took out a lighter and set fire to the list he had just made. He dropped the burning paper in an ashtray and watched it curl and blacken.

He poured another glass. As he sipped, he had an uneasy thought. What would happen if the disease got loose? Gutenberg must know what he had and only a madman would unleash such a terrible weapon. One of the reasons the Korean lab had been raided was to take that potential out of the hands of North Korea's unstable leader. At least, that's what Vysotsky had been told. The plague was safer in Russian hands. If it added to the Federation's arsenal of bio-weapons, so much the better.

He put the thought aside. Time to begin looking for the traitor.

CHAPTER 18

Lights on the corners of Krivi's laboratory buildings cast a bright glare into the night, reflecting from the harsh white of the snow covering the grounds. There was no moon. The sky was filled with dark, unseen cloud and the scent of a coming storm lay heavy in the night air.

Nick and the others had parked a quarter of a mile away. They were dressed in black and armed with the MP-5s and pistols. The C-4 and detonators were in a pack Nick would carry once they got out of the car.

"Those lights are a problem," Nick said.

"Once we're a little closer, I can take care of that," Ronnie said.

"You got something in your bag of tricks?" Lamont asked.

Ronnie held up an odd looking device shaped like a radar gun.

"This puts out a focused EMP burst. It's simple, point and shoot. Aim at the light, and out she goes. No sound to bother anyone."

"One of Langley's toys?"

"Yup. You know, we should have our own shop for stuff like this. Harker could set it up where we practice urban targets. There's plenty of room."

The metal building across from Project headquarters was used to practice live fire against electronic targets that popped out of rooms and mock buildings and alleys at random places and intervals. The shooter had to make an instant decision. Friend or foe? It was easy to mistake a toaster or a baby for a bomb, a beer bottle for a gun.

There were a lot of dead, fake civilians in that building, though there were a lot fewer than when the range had first been set up.

"'ll talk to Harker about it," Nick said. "Steph would appreciate another techie type to talk to."

He unfolded a set of plans for the ground floor of the lab and spread it out across his lap and clicked on a small flashlight. In the back seat, Lamont and Selena leaned over to look.

"This wing at the far end still looks like the best bet for entry," Nick said. He moved the light over the page.

"No windows, so no one sees us from inside. There's one exit door, on the far side away from the main entrance. Cameras on the corners. With Ronnie's gadget we can take out the cameras and the lights without knocking out the lights up front. If we're lucky, no one will notice. On the other hand, the guards will be at a monitoring station. If they're paying attention, they'll come looking to see what's up when the cameras go out."

"Rules of engagement?" Selena asked.

"It's a hard call. They may not know what's going on in there. Take them out but try not to kill them. If they start shooting, all bets are off."

"What if the samples aren't there?"

"Then we get the hell out of Dodge and come up with a new plan," Nick said. "But I'll bet they are."

"Let's get it done," Lamont said.

They pulled on black balaclavas against the cold and to conceal their faces from any cameras.

"Weapons free," Nick said.

They moved out of the car, black ghosts against the white countryside. The road was deserted. Snow was starting to fall, thick, heavy flakes that stuck to their clothes. They ran in a low crouch to the wall bordering the grounds. Ronnie settled behind the wall, pointed his EMP device at the nearest camera and pulled the trigger. He did the same to the camera on the far corner. Then he aimed at the nearest light. It went dark, with a soft pop. He followed up with the second. It went dark.

"Neat," Nick said. "Go."

They scrambled over the wall and ran to the back of the windowless wing. The entry door was made of metal. It had no window. It was marked with a large triangle and the universal bio-hazard sign with its three sharp-pointed open circles.

"Must be the right place," Lamont said.

Ronnie knelt before the lock with his tools. In a moment it was open. They stepped inside and closed the door.

"What is this place?" Selena said. "This doesn't look like a lab."

They were in a large room lit by fluorescent lights set in a row along the middle of the ceiling. There was a closed door at the far end. A stack of six refrigerated lockers took up part of one wall. The lockers hummed. The room smelled of disinfectant and conditioned air. It was cold.

Next to the lockers was a gleaming steel gurney wheels. A large, gray furnace with a steel door took up one corner. A chimney rose from the top and disappeared through the ceiling.

"Why do they need a big furnace like that in here?" Ronnie said.

"Explains the chimney outside," Nick said. "I don't know why."

In the center of the room was a glass cubicle. Inside the cubicle was a stainless metal table bolted to the floor. There was a drain underneath it and a hose hanging on a pivoting rack above. A rolling tray with shiny steel implements was placed neatly by the table.

"I think I know what this room is," Selena said. "It's a morgue. They must dispose of dead test animals in here. Do autopsies."

Nick walked to the lockers and opened a door.

"Shit," he said.

Ronnie walked over next to him. "Not just animals," he said.

Human feet lay behind the door. It was hard to tell if they belonged to a man or a woman. The feet were black and crusted, swollen and distorted. Several toes were missing.

"Close the damn door," Nick said.

"They're using humans as test subjects." Selena's face was white under the ski mask. "It explains the furnace. They must burn the bodies when they're done."

"Are we exposed because we opened that locker?" Lamont asked.

"I don't know," Nick said. "I don't think so. If the bodies were still contagious there'd be more safety protocols in place. It looks like they're only concerned when they open them up. In that cubicle." He pointed at the glass room.

"Let's find those samples and get out of here," Ronnie said. "This place gives me the creeps."

The door at the end of the room was unlocked. They stepped out of the morgue into a dimly lit hallway.

"I don't see any cameras," Nick said.

Ronnie took out a spray can from his bag and sent a long cloud of white dust into the hall. Halfway down the hall, a green line appeared at ankle height.

"Laser trip wire," he said.

Six doors lined this end of the hall, three on each side. A window was set in each door. They looked in the first room. It looked like a cubicle from an ICU in a modern hospital. The bed was surrounded by a clear plastic enclosure. The room was empty.

"That looks like an isolation unit," Selena said.

"These rooms must be where they keep their test subjects before they die," Nick said. His mouth was set in a tight line. They moved forward. Ronnie sprayed again and they stepped over the laser alarm.

They came to a junction. The hall formed the top part of a T. Straight ahead led toward the front of the building. To the left was a short hall and another door marked with the triangle and pronged circles.

"Bingo," Nick said. "We go in, verify it's the right place and ID the samples."

"How do we do that?" Selena asked.

"There has to be something. The Koreans called it E495. Whatever they call it here, it has to be labeled."

Ronnie sprayed again. "Another one." He pointed at a laser line across the hall. "They should have stuck with cameras. I still don't see any."

They stepped over the beam and entered the lab.

*****

The guard station for the laboratory building was located on the second floor, out of sight of prying eyes. There had never been a need for more than one man at night. It wasn't necessary. If there was a breach, a response in force was not far away.

Hans Kepler was studying a photograph in a Swedish porn magazine and failed to notice when the cameras went dark at the far end of the building. It wasn't until the door to the disposal wing opened and a soft alarm signaled intruders that he realized there was a problem. The magazine fell to the floor, forgotten. Hans studied the images from the hidden cameras on his screen.

Four pros. Armed.

He picked up his phone and dialed the emergency number.

"We have a breach," he said.

"How many?" The voice at the other end was impersonal.

"Four. They look military, black gear, machine pistols. They're carrying something in a pack. Right now they're in the disposal wing. They opened a locker."

"All right. We'll be there in ten. Wait for us."

"Don't worry. I'm not getting paid to be a hero."

"Ten minutes," the voice said, and disconnected.

CHAPTER 19

The door with the bio-hazard sign opened onto a long room and a state of the art laboratory. Like the morgue, there were no windows. Florescent lights illuminated the room in a cold, harsh glow. Nick recognized centrifuges and something he was pretty sure was an electron microscope. There were other instruments whose purpose was a mystery to him. Three stainless steel refrigerators stood against one wall. Next to them was a bulky gray filing cabinet. At the back of the lab was a glass cabinet, a sealed airlock and a large viewing window.

"Ronnie, you and Lamont start setting charges," Nick said. He took bricks of C-4 and a handful of detonators from his pack and handed them out. "Selena, you keep an eye on the door. I'm going to see what's in that filing cabinet."

"What about the samples? You want to blow the place up if we don't find them?" Selena said.

"Damn right I do. This has to be the right place. You saw that body back there."

Selena went to the door and stood near it, her MP-5 held close and ready. Nick walked to the filing cabinet. He tried a drawer. It was locked.

"Hey Ronnie. Let Lamont do the rest of that. I need you to open this lock."

Ronnie came over and took out his picks. It took less than a minute. Nick opened the top drawer.

"File folders," he said.

"What did you expect? It's a filing cabinet."

"They're labeled in German."

He pulled one out. It was labeled *Testpersonen.*

"You take the door," Nick said. "I need Selena to translate."

When Selena came over she looked at the folder Nick held in his hand.

"It says *Test Subjects*."

"How about this one?"

"*Schwarze Rose*. It means black rose."

She took it from him and looked at the first page.

"What does it say?"

"Black rose is a codename. These are notes about the plague."

"All right. We'll take these with us and read them later. See if there are any others you think we ought to grab. We can't take them all."

Nick left her looking through the files and went to the glass window at the back of the room. On the other side of the window was a bio containment unit. An air hose hung in yellow spirals over a work table from a rack on the ceiling. There was a door to the side that Nick assumed led into a decontamination area. The work table was clear, empty.

He walked over to the glass cabinet. The glass was thick and the cabinet door was secured with an electronic lock and keypad. Inside was a neat row of glass vials. He couldn't read the labels, but he could see that a second door on the other side of the cabinet opened into the containment room.

He took out another pack of C-4 and molded it against the glass.

"All done," Lamont said. "Ready to rock and roll."

Nick took out the radio controller for the detonators. "I'm giving it ten minutes. Mark."

He set the unit down by the containment room. Red numerals on the display began counting down the time.

"Let's get out of here."

He reached up to tug on his scarred left ear. It was beginning to itch. The itching got worse.

Nick's ear was a psychic warning system, a genetic hand me down from his Irish Ancestors. His grandmother had what the old Irish called "the sight." She'd been able to know about things that hadn't happened, bad things, death, accidents, disaster. It had made her unpopular in her small village.

Whatever it was or wherever it had come from, Nick had learned to trust it.

Ronnie saw him pull on his ear. They all knew what it meant.

"Oh, oh," he said.

"Turn off the lights," Nick said.

Selena swept her hand across a bank of switches on the wall next to the door. The room went dark. The only light was the red glow of the timer at the far end, counting down the minutes and seconds until this room would cease to exist.

Nick cracked the door open. The hall outside was empty. His ear began burning.

"Trouble coming," he said. He kept his voice low. "Time to boogie."

They moved to the T where the hall met the longer corridor that led back to the morgue and forward to the front of the building. Nick heard a soft sound toward the front, the barest whisper of something. He signaled with his hand. *That way. Someone coming.*

He signaled again. *Ronnie, with me. Selena, Lamont, cover the way we came in. On three.*

Nick held up his hand and counted off with his fingers. *One. Two. Three.*

He looked around the corner. Eight or nine men in dark blue uniforms, with MP-5s, coming from the front.

The leader saw Nick and shouted. His gun came up. Nick fired first. The leader went down and Nick ducked back as the hall filled with the sharp sounds of the guns and the whisper of bullets passing.

Lamont crouched low and fired around the corner. Selena reached her gun around the wall and fired blindly.

Behind them, the counter ticked down toward the explosion.

Ronnie reached into his bag and pulled out a flash bang.

"This will help them think. Cover up," he said.

He pulled the pin and tossed the grenade into the hall. It went off with a flat, hard sound. The shock wave beat against them in the narrow confines of the hall.

After-images of light danced in front of Nick's eyes. They moved into the main corridor. Blue-clad attackers writhed on the floor, hands clapped over their ears. Two still stood, disoriented. They raised their weapons. Nick and Selena shot them.

"Toward the back," Nick said.

They ran down the hall and into the morgue. Nick pulled open the outer door and was met with a blast of cold air and snow. The weather had turned into a full blown winter storm. Nick looked at his watch.

"Thirty seconds," he said.

They ran through the door, silhouetted by the lights in the room behind. Sudden spurts of flame winked at them from the dark. A heavy blow knocked Nick down into a drift. The others dove for the ground. Ronnie fired at the muzzle blast of the unseen shooter. A cry of pain cut through the muffled sound of the storm and the flashes stopped.

The charges went off.

The night erupted with flame and noise and light that turned the falling snow bright yellow and orange. The roof lifted off the building. The tall chimney toppled and crashed to the ground near where Selena and Lamont lay flat in the snow. Debris fell back to earth, chunks of masonry, bits of metal and glass, unidentifiable pieces. A mangled centrifuge landed next to Nick and lay steaming in the snow.

The light and noise faded. No one was shooting at them. A burning gas line sent a twenty foot column of bluish flame straight into the air from the ruined building behind them.

Nick stood up, holding his side. His vest had taken the round. But it hurt.

"Come on," he said.

"You're all right?" Selena asked.

"Yeah. Let's get out of here."

They made it back to the car without trouble. Selena drove. Nick sat next to her. They looked at the burning building as they passed it.

"They won't be using that for a while," Nick said.

CHAPTER 20

"What? Destroyed?"

Krivi had been called out of a sound sleep to answer the phone. He held it close to his ear and pulled his silk bathrobe around him as he listened to the voice on the other end of the line. The green numerals on the clock by his bedside read 3:21. The voice repeated what it had said. Krivi rubbed his chest and took a deep breath.

"All right. We'll put it out that it was a terrorist attack. That always satisfies everyone's need to know who was behind something. There must be plenty of evidence to support the idea. Look for anything that might tell us who did it. Anything at all."

More noise on the telephone.

"No. Stall the police. Access has to be controlled. Get our people there now. I'll talk to the commissioner and get his cooperation. Call me if there are problems."

He hung up and thought for a moment. It was a secured line, no one would have intercepted the conversation. He picked up the phone and dialed a number known only to six others.

"Yes." Gutenberg's voice was alert, though Krivi knew he'd been asleep. A call on this line at night meant trouble.

"We have a problem."

"Go on."

"Someone raided the lab where we had the Korean samples. It was a professional operation. They eliminated my security team and blew up the building."

"A military op?"

"Possibly. My team was the best. The Russians, perhaps."

"I would have been warned. It couldn't have been them," Gutenberg said.

"Then we'd better find out who it was."

"What about the vaccine? The test?"

"I'm going to talk with Schmidt after we're done here," Krivi said. "He has backups of his research and more samples of the bacteria stored in another location. This is a setback, nothing more. It will delay implementation, but in the end it won't make any difference."

"What about the police?"

"They won't be a problem."

"Let me know if you find anything to tell us who did it."

"Of course."

After a few more words, Krivi broke the connection. He leaned back in his chair and knew he'd never get back to sleep. He was offended that someone would dare to attack him. Eventually he'd discover who had done it and when he found out who they were, they were going to regret the day they were born.

CHAPTER 21

The snow was letting up by the time they got back to the safe house.

"Man, I'm beat," Lamont said. He sat down on a couch.

"You're getting old, Shadow," Ronnie said.

"I wouldn't talk about old if I were you," Lamont said. "You look a little worn out yourself."

Ronnie's face showed the strain of the raid. It hadn't been that long since he'd been lying in a hospital, near death.

"How you feeling, Ronnie?" Nick said.

"I'm fine."

"Get some sleep. Unless the snow closes the airport, we're out of here in the morning."

In their room, Selena helped Nick take off his vest.

"Ow," he said.

He unbuttoned his shirt. Selena helped him take it off, then worked his tee shirt up over his head. His side was a massive blotch of bruised color.

"Rainbow man," Selena said. "Very impressive. Any ribs broken?"

"I don't think so, but it feels like I got hit by a truck. Everything's stiffening up."

"It will feel better in the morning," she said.

"No it won't, but thanks for the thought."

"You could have been killed."

"That's what the vests are for. Good thing it was only one round, though."

"Do you think we stopped them tonight?"

"I don't know," Nick said. "We sure as hell slowed them down."

"People like them shouldn't be allowed to exist," she said. Her voice was touched with anger.

"There's always someone like them."

"That's the problem, isn't it? There's always someone who wants to run the world their way and who'll do anything to get what they want."

"At least this time we know who they are and where they live. We didn't stop AEON before, but we didn't know as much. Maybe this time around we can finish it."

"Adam and his group tried to stop them for centuries," Selena said. "They couldn't do it."

"They didn't have us to help them out," Nick said.

Selena laughed.

"Ah, hell, I'm tired," Nick said. "All I want is to get under that nice warm quilt on the bed over there. With you."

"That's all?"

"Well, maybe not."

He leaned over and kissed her. They held it for a long minute. She reached up and pulled him closer.

"Ow," he said again.

"You sure about the bed? I thought you said you were tired. And you're hurting."

"What's a little pain between friends? And I'm not that tired."

Later, after he was asleep, she stared at the ceiling for a long time. Next to her, his body radiated heat like a furnace. She thought about what he'd said about Adam, about his group not having the team to help in the past.

He was serious, she thought. *People have been trying to bring down AEON for a thousand years and he thinks that we're the ones to do it. He meant it, it's how he thinks of himself, of the team. He means to take them down.*

Outside the window of the bedroom, the wind was dying out. They'd be able to leave tomorrow and it couldn't be soon enough for her. She'd always loved the Alps, but after tonight she didn't think Switzerland would ever feel the same.

How did I get here?

She stared up at the ceiling for a long time.

CHAPTER 22

Valentina Antipov waited until Gutenberg's snoring was in full flower before she got out of bed. She looked at him with distaste. He'd been particularly clumsy tonight and it had taken all her considerable skills to convince him of his romantic prowess. She picked up a red silk nightgown from the floor by the bed, slipped it on and padded softly into the other room.

Gutenberg's laptop computer sat on a desk by the window. It was password protected, of course, but Valentina had long ago discovered the key, a combination of his wife's name and his birth date. For all his power and intelligence, Gutenberg was naive about things like passwords. It would never occur to him that his not-so-intelligent mistress would even look at his computer, much less be able to access the files on it. He should have been using a biometric security lock, but he'd once told her he didn't trust them. Biometrics had been known to fail.

Valentina enjoyed making a fool of him. It was one of the pleasures of her job.

Something had happened to upset him. She didn't know what it was, but she knew it was important. Johannes had flown in to Paris unexpectedly and ordered her to be ready for him later in the day. A business meeting, he'd said, but then he'd be free. He'd sounded strained over the phone, even worried, angry. She had never known him to be worried about anything.

Valentina had decided to look at the laptop and see if she could find out why Gutenberg was here, or who it was he'd met with. There was little risk she'd be discovered. His snores echoed loudly in the other room.

Half a bottle of cognac will do that to you, she thought. *Pig.*

An ornate iron street lamp cast soft, yellow light over snow dusting the cobbled street outside the window. This part of Paris still had the feel of the old city, the Paris of van Gogh and Matisse, of Voltaire and Moliere. Valentina loved Paris. As much as she missed the sounds and nightlife of her native Moscow, she had to admit it was nothing like the city of light.

The sounds in the other room stopped and Valentina froze where she was. A moment later, they started again. She took a deep breath and opened the computer. She entered the password. The screen filled with fifty or sixty file icons, like miniature file folders. Gutenberg was obsessive about records. There was probably a psychological term for it, but she didn't know what it was. He always kept a record of anything he thought important.

If there was something that could tell her what had upset Gutenberg, it would be a recent entry. There was no time to look into each folder. Most of them would be business files, of interest but little use to her. She wanted something recent.

She moved the cursor over the folders, pausing only to see the date of entry. She came to a folder marked K. The entry date was the night before. She clicked on the file. Flashing red letters appeared on the screen.

ENTER CODE

Damn!

That had never happened before.

Her purse lay on a chair nearby. She went to it and took out a high speed flash drive given to her by SVR's technicians and went back to the computer. She inserted it and copied Gutenberg's entire drive without trying to crack the code on the file. She shut down the computer, withdrew the device and put it back in her purse.

Let Moscow worry about it, she thought. She'd arrange for it to get to the embassy tomorrow, after Gutenberg was gone.

Her work done, Valentina slipped back into bed. She looked over at the man sleeping next to her.

Men are such fools, she thought.

CHAPTER 23

"I like it," Nick said.

"You do?"

Nick and Selena stood in the empty space of a converted loft building overlooking the Potomac and Robert E. Lee's beloved Virginia.

The loft was on the top floor of an eight story brick warehouse that had been a clothing factory at the turn of the 20th century. The machines, cutting tables and bales of raw cloth were long gone. No one from that time would have imagined the change that had come to the building.

The original floors of oak had been sanded smooth, stained and finished to perfection until they glowed with warm light. A row of tall, paned windows faced out onto the river. The bricks had been exposed and finished along one wall. Light poured into the loft through skylights placed along the high ceiling. The space had been partitioned with an architect's skill into a great room, master bedroom, a large study/library and two guest rooms. There were two and a half bathrooms. There was a gas fireplace in the living area and the master bedroom. Overhead lights were recessed into the ceiling.

The walls were painted off-white. The loft was a blank canvas, ready for whatever imagination its new owners could bring to it.

"What do you think?" Nick asked. He walked over to one of the windows. His footsteps echoed in the empty space. A line of barges was passing on the river, shepherded by two large tugs.

"I like it too," Selena said.

"Then let's take it."

"You're sure?"

"I'm sure."

"Then we should go see the agent."

"We need to talk about how we pay for it," Nick said.

It was a conversation Selena knew was coming. "Nick..."

"Hear me out," he said. "I know you can pay for it. I don't want you to."

"Why not? I have more than enough, you know that. What good is money if you can't spend it on what you want?"

"There are plenty of things you can spend it on here, if that's what you want," Nick said. "But this has to be a 50/50 deal. You cover half, I cover half."

"This place is expensive."

"So? It's not like that place you're in now. We'll take out a mortgage like everybody else. That way it will be ours. I think it's important."

Stubborn, Selena thought. *Why not just let me handle it?* But she knew why. It would never work between them if she paid for everything.

"What about your apartment?" she asked.

"The lease runs for another year. I have a sublet clause. There's not going to be a problem finding someone to take it over."

He put his arm around her. She leaned against him and looked out over the water.

"It's a beautiful space," she said. "It will be fun to decorate it."

"Too bad there's no furniture here now."

"What do you mean?"

"I was thinking of the bedroom."

"I'm thinking about couches and rugs and you're thinking about that? The bed?"

"Who said anything about a bed? I was thinking about the Klee you gave me, the one in my bedroom. It will look great over the fireplace."

She looked at him. He was grinning.

"Liar," she said.

CHAPTER 24

The clinic was in an impoverished village named Sao Benedito, a tiny dot located on the edge of the Raposa Serra do Sol Indian Reservation in the northernmost tip of Brazil. The village consisted of about forty houses built from mud, wood and palm leaves. Behind the houses were garden plots and a few animals kept by the villagers for milk and food. Most of the villagers eked out a minimal existence as farmers. The clinic treated a variety of infections and injuries brought on by work, nature and too much *cachaca* at the local bar on a weekend night.

The Indians lived on a vast tract of tropical forest, rivers, broad savannahs and tall mountains. It was a beautiful place, a hunting and fishing paradise. With the beauty came danger and the possibility of sudden, unpleasant death. Poisonous snakes and insects, giant spiders, vampire bats and the occasional jaguar made life interesting. The people who lived on the reservation came to the clinic for emergency treatment when the traditional healing ways had failed. The government stayed away from the area as much as possible and the village was remote. In short, it was perfect for Karl Schmidt's needs.

Schmidt loved field work. He was an avid outdoorsman, hiking the mountains near Zürich as often as possible. Krivi indulged him with a month's holiday each year, a European tradition that Schmidt used to book travel to exotic locations. He'd never been to Brazil and had been looking forward to it. The beauty of the land was better than he'd hoped for. It was secondary, of course. He hadn't come to sightsee.

He'd come to kill.

The destruction of the laboratory in Zürich had speeded up Karl's schedule. Backups of the modified plague and three hundred doses of the trial vaccine had been stored at Krivi's corporate headquarters, where several floors were given over to research labs developing new products for Dass Pharmaceuticals. More samples of the vaccine and the plague had been shipped to Krivi's manufacturing labs in Mumbai.

All the bureaucratic details required by the Brazilian authorities to begin the inoculation program had been completed before the Zürich attack. In a way, the destruction of the lab had acted as a spur to move forward. Karl would have preferred a few more weeks of testing but the raid took the decision from him. Krivi and Gutenberg had become impatient after the explosion. Schmidt was in Brazil only to supervise the start of the trial. Even though he'd been injected with the vaccine, he intended to be far away by the time the plague showed itself.

The first signs were fever and a severe headache. Then came high fever, sneezing and coughing as the disease attacked the lungs and entered the contagious stage. By day six after exposure, the patient was unable to stand or eat and the internal organs were breaking down. The characteristic flower-shaped black blotches appeared. By day eight, most who'd been infected were dead. No one had ever lasted longer than ten days. But for three days after exposure, everything would seem normal.

It was possible the disease would spread beyond the village and the reservation, but the place was remote enough that it was unlikely. Even if it did, access to the area was limited. A quarantine wouldn't prove difficult. If it did go out of control, a Brazil destabilized by an epidemic wasn't necessarily a bad thing.

Outside the clinic the first patients of the morning waited. It was a gorgeous day.

"We're ready, Herr Schmidt."

The speaker was Doctor Silva, a stocky man with honey-colored skin and a high pitched voice that didn't seem to go with his body. He gestured at a table laid out with neat rows of disposable hypodermic syringes filled with clear fluid.

"It's a wonderful thing, what you are doing for our people, " Silva said.

"It's nothing," Schmidt said. "Our company believes in giving something back. This is our way of doing it."

Doctor Silva believed he was injecting a new product that would be effective against a deadly, drug resistant strain of malaria that had found its way to the region. That part was true. Every tenth dose also carried the plague bacilli. Schmidt had made sure Silva received the vaccine. He needed the doctor to survive and report the results.

"Shall we get started?" Schmidt said.

The first patients were a woman from the reservation and her two children. Schmidt had something of a soft spot for children. It was too bad so many of them would die, but it couldn't be helped. Besides, life expectancy was short here. Better an early death than years of poverty and misery. And what did these people have to look forward to? A primitive life of disease and isolation.

They contributed nothing. By dying, they would prove useful.

Their deaths would fertilize the seeds of the new world order.

CHAPTER 25

Elizabeth had mixed feelings about the Zürich raid. On the surface, it looked like a success. The team had been in the right place. The plague-ridden corpses in the disposal room, the files they'd recovered and pictures of the lab proved that. The international papers were calling it a terrorist attack, although no one seemed to know why a pharmaceutical research lab had been targeted. The Swiss police were baffled and angry. Such things didn't happen in Switzerland. It was disorderly.

Although the samples in Zürich had been destroyed, she had a bad feeling that the plague was still in play. There was no firm evidence to make her believe that. It was a matter of intuition and years of experience. AEON was too clever to put all their resources in one place. The raid might have eliminated the threat but what if it hadn't?

The files recovered from the lab contained hard data and summarized research notes. The research notes weren't signed, but Elizabeth thought they were probably done by Karl Schmidt. She'd passed the file on to CDC in Atlanta. The file on the test subjects was gruesome and proved that human subjects had been used as guinea pigs. Twenty-seven had died before a new test batch of vaccine showed promise. Detailed autopsy reports and notes described the grim progress of the disease and it's inevitable outcome.

Things had moved past her resources and responsibility. She had proof that the plague was a genuine national security threat. She was on her way to the White House to brief the president.

Elizabeth's driver turned onto Pennsylvania Avenue and passed through new security barriers installed since the last time she'd been here. Secret Service agents met her at a side entrance and relieved her of her pistol. They gave her a visitor pass to hang around her neck and escorted her to the Oval Office, where President Rice was expecting her.

Rice was behind his desk. He was an average looking man at first glance. It was only on closer inspection that people were captured by the intensity in his eyes. They were blue with a hint of green and conveyed a sense of total attention when he looked at you. Like all who had held this office, he seemed surrounded by an intangible aura of power. Elizabeth had felt it before with other presidents. His face showed the strain of his job, here where there was no need to look good for the cameras and the public eye wasn't upon him.

Rice was not alone in the room. DCI Clarence Hood was present as well.

"Mister President, thank you for seeing me."

"Please take a seat, Director. I thought it best if Clarence sat in on this."

She nodded to him as she sat down. Clarence Hood had become a personal friend.

"Sir, I requested this meeting because I believe we are facing a threat unlike any we've dealt with before."

"That sounds ominous, Director," Rice said.

"You already know what we discovered from the papers of North Korea's defector. I followed up on that."

She briefed the two men on everything that had happened, ending with the raid on the Zürich laboratory.

"So that's why you wanted the safe house," Hood said.

"Why wasn't I told about this operation?" Rice said.

"Sir, that's why I'm here now. Until I had definite proof of what these people were doing, I felt you had no need to know."

"If the Swiss find out we're responsible, they'll make a lot of trouble."

"They won't find out, Mister President. I guarantee it."

"They better hadn't. You are certain it was the Russians that took the samples from the North Koreans?"

"Yes, sir, I am. We determined that through satellite surveillance. Then our source verified our finding before he was killed."

"This Adam person?"

"Yes, sir."

"Mm. Go on."

"Sir, there can only be one reason AEON subjected human subjects to this terrible disease. They are working to create a vaccine against it or have already done so."

Hood sighed. "You think they intend to release it."

"That's right," Elizabeth said. "It's a perfect terrorist weapon. There's no cure that we know of and it's always fatal."

"I can understand one of the fundamentalist groups wanting to do something like that," Rice said. "They hate everyone who doesn't believe as they do and they justify it as God's will. But why would a group of successful business men do such a thing? It doesn't make sense."

"I can only speculate on that," Elizabeth said. "AEON seems to want a world they can dominate and control. They've demonstrated that they have no concern for the cost in human life. I don't think they have any agenda beyond dominance."

"Amoral," Hood said.

"Totally. They have no ethical or moral considerations."

"Who else is part of this organization besides Gutenberg and Dass?" Rice asked.

"I can't answer that," Elizabeth said. "But we do know those two are leaders. Sir, the resources at my disposal aren't enough to tackle this by myself."

"I can set up full surveillance on Gutenberg and Dass, Mister President," Hood said. "They might lead us to the others."

"Do it," Rice said.

"Yes, sir."

"We could look into Gutenberg's finances," Elizabeth said. "Whatever else is going on, money must be part of it. Terrorist acts require funding. If we find a money trail, we can follow it. Dass is the one with the facilities to handle the samples and develop any vaccine or cure. We need to know what he's doing as well."

They waited as Rice considered what they'd said.

"All right," he said. "I want this kept between the two of you. Spying on foreign nationals influential in finance and industry is a mine field, politically speaking. We get enough flak about surveillance as it is from our supposed allies. They don't like us finding out when they act against our interests."

"If they don't like it, perhaps they should stop doing it," Hood said.

"Make sure the media never hears you say that," Rice said. "I'd hate to lose you."

CHAPTER 26

The windows of Alexei Vysotsky's office looked out across the Yasenevo District outside of Moscow, all the way to the golden onion domes of the Kremlin. In summer, hundreds of trees made a sea of leafy green stretching all the way to the river. In the winter, as now, the bare branches revealed the grimy urban sprawl surrounding the modern office building that housed Russia's Foreign Intelligence Service.

The sun cast watery light from a thin curtain of high, cold sky. Outside, the temperature hovered somewhere below zero. Vysotsky's office was hot and stuffy. He sat at his desk with his collar open and cursed the engineers who had designed a system that roasted you or left you in freezing cold.

The temperature of the room was the least of Vysotsky's concerns. He'd just finished reading a summary of the contents of Gutenberg's encrypted drive. Valentina had sent him a headache of the first order. He opened the bottom drawer of his desk, took out the vodka and poured a drink. He downed half, topped off the glass, and put the bottle back. Then he opened the report on Gutenberg's computer.

The material was an intelligence officer's dream, a treasure trove of names, numbers and personal observations. There were two encrypted files. The first was a private journal. Alexei couldn't believe a man so powerful would be so careless as to keep a record like this. It was more than a diary. It was as if Gutenberg was making notes for future generations, a kind of contemporary history. If the material was a dream, it was also a nightmare. Alexei had a big problem on his hands, big enough to destroy him if he wasn't careful.

3 February

The Korean samples have been procured. The information Kamarov obtained from his nephew was perfect. His men had no trouble with the train or the guard detachment. No witnesses. No casualties on our side. The samples will be in Zürich tomorrow.

Konstantine Kamarov, Vysotsky thought, *and his bastard nephew Vladimir. Traitors, both of them. They killed my men.*

A sudden wave of anger swept through him. If Kamarov had been in the room, Alexei would have wrapped his hands around the man's fat throat and squeezed until blood ran out of his eyes.

A dull pounding in Vysotsky's head signaled that his blood pressure was heading for the roof. He forced himself to take a breath and relax. It wouldn't help to give himself a stroke.

Konstantine Kamarov was one of the most powerful men in the Federation, one of the Oligarchs who'd come out of the darkness after the collapse of the Soviet Union. His nephew was Vladimir Kamarov, Deputy Director of SVR and Vysotsky's boss.

I need to make sure his loving nephew doesn't find out about this file, Vysotsky thought. *I'll tell him about it just before I put a bullet in the back of his head.*

The second encrypted file outlined a plan to test the virulent plague in Brazil before releasing it on a wider scale in China. It cited examples from history and modern times of what happened when a country's medical infrastructure failed and life-threatening disease spread among the population. There was a detailed analysis of how Gutenberg's consortium of banks could provide the loans required to finance recovery and establish dominance. The graphs and charts were convincing. The profit margins and net gains were impressive. The document projected two hundred million deaths in China alone and discussed the costs of cleaning up the aftermath. An addendum to the file discussed how much profit could be made from sales of the vaccine.

Vysotsky finished his drink and poured another. He was a man hardened by years of working as an officer in one of the most brutal and secretive intelligence organizations that had ever existed. He'd seen many things in his career, but nothing to match the pure evil of what Gutenberg was planning.

The man's a monster, Vysotsky thought, *but perhaps I can take advantage of what he has created.*

Russia was not mentioned in the plan. It made sense that Gutenberg and Kamarov wouldn't want to disrupt the enormous income that flowed to them through manipulation of Russian industry and oil contracts. Kamarov controlled everything from the production of the new MIG fighter planes to the knockoff American blue jeans sold on the street corners of Moscow.

Vysotsky read further in Gutenberg's journal.

23 February

Talked with K. in Zürich. Progress! Schmidt is a genius. He's ready to test a possible vaccine. Everything had been made ready previously at K.'s bioresearch lab, in anticipation of obtaining the samples. Kamarov's plan to persuade the Kremlin to authorize the raid on the North Koreans saved us a lot of trouble.

Volunteers have signed up and test subjects chosen. Facilities have been ready for several weeks, including the necessary crematorium.

Who is K.? Vysotsky wondered. The next entry was about a dinner party and the menu, of no importance. It was the entry after that that sounded alarms for Vysotsky, even more than learning of Kamarov's treachery.

27 February

The teleconference with the others went well. Everyone is pleased. Mitchell pointed out that Washington's reaction to the outbreak of plague would be denial that any problem existed for the U.S. He suggested that after the initial wave of reports had passed, the media should play up the wonders of American healthcare. Reports of the severity of the plague could be suppressed until deaths had reached some critical number, perhaps fifty or sixty thousand. Then a fear-based campaign could be launched to encourage Americans to line up for vaccinations.

There was general agreement to do this in each of our respective spheres of influence.

De Guillame pointed out that the outbreak would provide a perfect opportunity to test our new nano-trackers. Each tracker would be digitally

*imprinted on the spot via secure wireless
connection with the name, address and government
ID number of the person receiving a vaccination.
It's a good idea, but the manufacturing facility is
not ready yet.*

*A motion was raised and seconded to table the
discussion on the trackers until a later date. It was
carried unanimously.*

*This was followed by a general discussion.
Thorvaldson and Halifax think we should focus on
stimulating a backlash against immigration prior to
releasing the plague. Mitchell laughed and said
there was already plenty of backlash in his country.
Halifax agreed that every western nation and many
in other parts of the world were well primed to turn
against the inferior races attempting to infiltrate
and undermine our societies. It was agreed that we
will ramp up immigration issues in our respective
nations in preparation for severe government
restrictions, using the plague as an excuse.*

The report was succinct, thorough and
professional. It had been prepared by an officer
named Ilya Yezhov. Vysotsky pulled up Yezhov's
file on his computer.

Yezhov was thirty years old. He'd graduated
from the Moscow Military Commanders School
with high honors and been commissioned a Junior
Lieutenant. A year later he'd put in a request for
Spetsnaz training and been accepted. Yezhov had
served with distinction in Chechnya, where he'd
been promoted and awarded the Medal for Courage
for bravery in combat. He'd been brought into
Zaslon three years before and promoted to his
present rank of Captain. Yezhov had taken a
specialized internal SVR training in sophisticated

surveillance techniques and cyber warfare, which was why Gutenberg's drive had landed on his desk for evaluation. For once the system had gotten it right the first time.

Vysotsky gave a grunt of approval. He depressed a switch on his intercom.

"Yes, General."

"Find Captain Ilya Yezhov and get him here."

"At once, General." The voice sounded as though it had snapped to attention.

While he waited, Alexei thought about what he'd just read. A group of powerful men. It was all so depressingly familiar. He wondered if it was the same group again, AEON in a new configuration. Over the last two years they'd caused a lot of trouble, but he thought they had been destroyed. Perhaps this was a different group, perhaps not. It made no difference. Now that he had names, he'd soon know who they were. It was a given that they were all powerful and wealthy, like Kamarov. If he wasn't careful, Alexei knew they would crush him.

A sharp knock on his door announced Yezhov's arrival. Vysotsky reached down under his desk and activated a device that blanketed the room against any possible electronic surveillance.

"Come."

Yezhov was a taut, muscular man, a picture of how a Russian officer should look. His tall boots gleamed. His uniform was immaculate. Vysotsky would have expected nothing else, but it confirmed Yezhov's professionalism. The captain's face bore the mark of the Russian steppes, high cheekbones and dark brown eyes that matched his close cropped hair. He had a thin scar on the side of his jaw that ran back to his ear, a permanent reminder of his time in Chechnya. His lips were full, almost sensuous. He was about six feet tall. Yezhov was a man in his prime.

Yezhov saluted.

"Sir."

"At ease, Captain. Take that chair. Sit."

"Sir." Yezhov sat. His back was ramrod straight.

"I have been reading your report on the material discovered by our agent in Paris. You have been thorough."

"I try to be, sir."

"Have you spoken to anyone about this report?"

"No, sir.

"No one else knows what is in it?"

"No, General. The material is too sensitive. I was careful to maintain the highest security. You are the only person to see it."

Vysotsky nodded. "Good. What did you think of the contents? Give me your evaluation."

Alexei watched Yezhov carefully. It was a test. He was asking Yezhov to comment on explosive material that would create serious problems in the Kremlin and elsewhere. How would he respond? Would he evade? Hesitate? If he did, he was not the man Alexei wanted.

"Sir, if this information is accurate, it is critical we give it our full attention," Yezhov said. "It's bad enough that these men are planning an attack on nations vital to our national interest. It's worse that Konstantine Kamarov is one of them. He's a traitor. He should be arrested."

"I an certain the information is accurate, Captain. How would you approach the problem? Need I remind you that his nephew oversees our operations and appears to be responsible for the death of Major Kaminsky and his men?"

"With all due respect, sir, that is an obstacle that must be overcome. As to how I would go about it, I think a tactical solution is required. But I would proceed with great caution."

"A black operation?"

"Absolutely, sir. Blacker than the inside of a Siberian coal miner's ass."

"Your imagery is graphic, Captain. What would be the goal of such an operation?"

"Obtaining proof that Kamarov is a traitor and finding out more about this group."

"How would you obtain such proof?"

Yezhov paused, thinking. He seemed calm, at ease. Vysotsky waited, watching him. He was pleased by what he saw.

Not many could sit in front of me and keep their composure in a situation like this, he thought. *This is a man who knows who he is.*

"Kamarov is widely disliked," Yezhov began. "No one would be surprised if something happened to him. He knows this. I am sure he has heavy security with him everywhere he goes and at his residences."

Vysotsky nodded. "Continue."

"I don't think we can delay, sir, based on what's in that file. You asked how I would obtain proof. If he were to be kidnapped and a public ransom demand made, it would appear to be just another mafia extortion. Kamarov could be questioned in private about his plans. He'll give us proof."

"And then?"

Yezhov shrugged. "The man's a traitor. His body might provide an object lesson to others who consider betraying the Motherland."

"You would eliminate him, then."

"An excuse could be made that would satisfy everyone. Perhaps a communication from the supposed kidnappers."

"You would have done well in the old days, Captain. Prepare a detailed plan to put your idea into action. Have it on my desk by 0800 tomorrow."

It was an order and a dismissal. Yezhov stood.

"Yes, sir. Is that all, sir?"

Vysotsky waved his hand in the air, toward the door.

Yezhov saluted, turned in a precise half circle and left the room, closing the door after him.

Alexei got out the vodka and filled his glass. He'd just made the opening move in a dangerous game. If what he planned was discovered, he'd be finished. You didn't go after someone as powerful as Kamarov without risking everything. The oligarch would have serious men guarding him, former Spetsnaz who knew their job. Yezhov would have his work cut out for him.

Vysotsky sipped his vodka and thought about when he'd been a younger man. He missed the action of the old days, the fine adrenaline edge that came in the field, when everything hinged on one's planning, skill and luck. Now such things had passed to the next generation, although a bullet could as easily find him as a man like Yezhov. The only difference would be that his bullet would come while he was kneeling in some God-forsaken place instead of facing his enemies. Much had changed in Russia but some things would always be the same.

I'm coming for you, Comrade Kamarov.

Vysotsky raised his glass and smiled to himself. He hadn't felt this alive in years.

CHAPTER 27

Valentina Antipov sat inside the warmth of a corner café on the Place de la Bastille at a window table and watched the crowds scurry by outside. It was a sunny Saturday and Parisians were out in force. Valentina sipped her espresso and waited for her contact to arrive.

It was unusual for Vysotsky to set up a direct meeting. One never knew who'd been identified by the opposition as someone working for SVR. Every public contact like this ran the risk of exposure. She was certain no one knew who she was or that she worked for Vysotsky. The public atmosphere of the café provided a plausible cover for the meeting. All the same, she wasn't happy about it.

The Valentina Rosetti legend was as good as SVR's master forgers could make it. Her passport was an authentic Italian issue. A deeper probe would discover all the paperwork a young girl growing up in Italy would accumulate. In Italy, there was a lot of paperwork and a bureaucracy noted for resisting attempts to penetrate its official archives. It would be very difficult to prove she was anyone other than she was supposed to be.

The café was crowded and noisy and blue with smoke. The government ban on smoking indoors was sneered at by most of the French. She took out a package of Gitanes, withdrew a cigarette and lit it with a slim, gold lighter Johannes had given her. She smoked Gitanes as much because she liked the blue Deco design of a gypsy woman on the package as for the strong tobacco. She drew the smoke deep into her lungs, exhaled in a long stream and felt herself relax just a little.

Her contact entered the café and came across the room to her table. She knew him only as Lucien. It was all she needed to know.

Lucien leaned down, kissed her lightly on each cheek and sat down across from her. It was a scene repeated a thousand times a day in Paris. He looked like any well-off Parisian man, reasonably handsome, somewhere in his late 30s or early 40s. His suit was well cut of good material, the kind of suit that spoke of respectability and sufficient income to be a likely companion of the beautiful young woman sitting across from him.

"Cheri. Good to see you." He spoke to her in French

Valentina answered in the same language. "And you, Lucien."

A harassed waiter came by. Lucien ordered a croissant and coffee in rapid, impeccable French.

When he was gone, Lucien said, "Armand is pleased with your last report."

Armand was General Vysotsky.

"I'm glad to hear it."

"He would like you to do something for him."

Lucien reached into his jacket pocket and took out a small flash drive, no bigger than a thumbnail, and placed it on the table near her coffee cup. She lifted the coffee to her lips and palmed the drive at the same time.

Anyone watching would have seen only two lovers talking. Perhaps they were planning an evening at the theater. Perhaps he was asking her to his hotel room. Anything was possible in Paris, between a man and a woman having coffee in a café.

"Insert the drive into the computer that you copied for Armand," Lucien said.

"What does it do?"

"It will add a line of code that will allow us to intercept his communications. The computer must be on, of course. It only takes a minute. You'll see a progress bar on the screen. Get rid of the drive after it's done. "

"He usually keeps his laptop with him and it's always off except when he's working. It could be a problem."

"It wasn't a problem before," Lucien said. He smiled, but his voice was cold. "I'm sure you'll find another opportunity."

"As you say," Valentina said. She stubbed out her Gitane and lit another.

"How can you stand those?" Lucien said. "I much prefer American cigarettes."

"I like the flavor."

The waiter brought the coffee and croissant. Lucien took a bite of the pastry.

"I'm really quite fond of these," he said. "Somehow they don't taste quite the same outside of France. When is the next time he'll be here?"

There was no need for him to say who he was talking about.

"Tomorrow. He's coming in to meet with the directors of his French bank."

"Good." Lucien finished the croissant and wiped his lips with the back of his hand. "This man has become a priority. Get to that computer as quickly as possible."

CHAPTER 28

"How are we going to stop Gutenberg?" Elizabeth asked. Everyone was in her office.

"Can we get into his computer?" Nick said. "There could be something on it to tell us what they're doing."

"It depends," Stephanie said. "If it's online and I can find it, I can hack into it."

Stephanie was the Project's secret weapon. She had a gift with computers, one that couldn't be taught. No one could keep her out once she decided to get in. Sometimes it just took a little longer.

"I always wondered how you did that," Lamont said, "get past all the firewalls."

"How *do* you do it, Steph?" Selena asked.

"Do what?"

"Get past the encryption protocols."

"You really want to know? It's a little hard to explain."

"How about the short version?" Nick said. "I always wondered myself."

"Do you know what an RSA algorithm is?" Stephanie said.

"Doesn't it have something to do with prime numbers?" Selena asked.

"That's right. A prime number is something that can only be divided by one and by itself. Most encryption schemes use prime numbers in a mathematical formula. Basically, what you do is create two different keys based on your formula. There's a public key and a private key that have interlocking patterns. Anyone might know the public key. That's what you use to encrypt the message. The private key is used to decrypt it. Without the private key you can't understand the message, even if you intercept it. If you want your data to be secure, you apply your formula and the computer encodes it. Any data, not just messages back and forth."

"But couldn't someone with the right skills figure out the key by using some kind of pattern recognition program?" Selena asked.

Stephanie nodded. "That's right on the money. They could, except that whoever writes the program adds in something called a padding scheme to prevent exactly that. It injects random factors into the equation. That makes the message almost impossible to crack unless you have the private key."

"But you figured out how to do it," Lamont said.

"I did," Stephanie said. "It got me into a lot of trouble. When I was eighteen I hacked into the Pentagon just for fun. Two days later the FBI showed up at my door. Scared the hell out of me."

Everyone laughed.

Stephanie smiled. "Anyway, it worked out. Instead of throwing me in jail they gave me a job with NSA. That's where Elizabeth found me."

"That's a hell of a story," Ronnie said. "But I still don't understand how you do it."

"You can't expect a Marine to understand stuff like that," Lamont said.

Ronnie started to say something but Elizabeth cut him off.

"Shall we get back to the purpose of this meeting? Steph, I like Nick's idea. Can you do it?"

"I can get into Gutenberg's corporate computers," Stephanie said. "Those will be active all the time. His personal computers are a different story. I have to be able to intercept something when he's online. Then I can slip in a program that will let me access the computer any time it's turned on. From there I can break whatever encryption scheme that's running and read everything on it."

"You said intercept something. Like an email?"

"Yes."

"Then why don't we send our pal Gutenberg a message?" Nick said. "When he responds, you'll have him."

"That would work, but why would he respond?"

"I guess it depends on what you say."

"You could pretend to be someone he'd have to answer," Selena said.

Steph looked thoughtful. "Once I'm into his bank's server, I could send him a message from one of his executives. It would look right. Gutenberg would think it was legitimate and answer it. The computer he used would be mine after that."

"Keep it simple," Elizabeth said. "Once that's done, see what you can do about Krivi."

"So now we wait and see what Steph comes up with?" Nick asked.

"Now we wait," Elizabeth said.

CHAPTER 29

Stephanie bypassed the firewalls on Gutenberg's bank servers and sent an email to him. It appeared to come from the vice president of operations and required a reply. She'd tagged the message with an automatic alarm to alert her when Gutenberg answered. His response would be captured and traced back to his computer. He could hide his location in a hundred different ways, bounce the signal all over the world, but she would find him. Then she would only have to wait until he was online again to plant her Trojan horse.

As it happened, she got lucky. She was sitting in her office thinking about the problem of Krivi Dass when the alarm signaled a hit.

Got you, she thought.

She had to work fast, before he signed off. Her fingers flew over her keyboard as she backtracked the signal through a dozen false Internet addresses to the source. She tapped a key. Seconds later her lines of code had burrowed into Gutenberg's secure, personal computer. She entered another command. The contents of Gutenberg's hard drive began transferring to Virginia. She had almost all of it before he shut down.

She disconnected from the Internet and began looking at the files. A red warning notice flashed across her screen, triggered by a program she'd written to protect her laptop.

UNAUTHORIZED ACCESS DETECTED.
CONTINUE? Y/N

The files she'd downloaded were isolated from any outside source. The security warning indicated an intruder on Gutenberg's computer, not hers. Someone else had been looking at the files at the same time she was.

She entered Y and thought about what the warning notice meant.

Given the level of security wrapped around Gutenberg's machine, whoever was watching him had to have a high level of experience dealing with sophisticated encryption schemes. Very few could do that. She could count the number of individuals who might be able to pull it off on one hand. The only other possibility was a government agency.

Sooner or later, whoever had the skill to break into Gutenberg's computer would discover the program she'd planted to monitor his communications. If they were really good, they would trace the program back to Virginia. They would never break through the encryption protocols Stephanie had created to protect the Project computers. But they would know where those computers were.

That was the bad news. The good news was that it worked both ways. With a little effort she could find out who was watching him and where they were, or at least where their server was located. She activated a digital hall of mirrors that would defeat any attempts to access her computer, went online and began following the trail. Ten minutes later she had her answer. She stood and went into Elizabeth's office.

"Got a minute? Something's come up."

"Come on in," Elizabeth said. "I was just thinking about Gutenberg and what we might do about him."

Dark shadows under her eyes stood out on Elizabeth's milk white skin. Her elfin features seemed stressed, as if she were listening to an unpleasant sound she couldn't avoid.

"Things just got a little more complicated," Stephanie said.

"How so?"

"I got into Gutenberg's computer and managed to download most of what was on it."

"And?"

"I don't know what's in those files yet, but I found a program a lot like mine. Someone else has the same idea we do."

"Someone else is spying on him?" Elizabeth said. "Who is it?"

"That's where it gets more complicated. It's someone working out of SVR headquarters in Yasenevo."

"The Russians." Elizabeth sighed.

"Yes. SVR is monitoring Gutenberg's computer just like I was."

"Do they know you were there?"

"They might," Stephanie said. "It depends on how they've got it set up on their end. I think we should assume they'll notice my trace. SVR will figure it out. They'll know it's us."

"You were right when you said it just got more complicated."

Elizabeth picked up her pen and began tapping it on the desk.

"If SVR is monitoring Gutenberg, they know he's the one who took those plague samples. Adam told Nick that it was Vysotsky's group that lost them. I know how Vysotsky thinks. He's going to want to get the samples back and extract revenge for his men. Plus his head's probably on the chopping block if he doesn't manage to contain this."

"He's got some shot at coming up with the samples," Stephanie said.

Elizabeth laid her pen down and pushed it away as if it might bite her. "Have you tapped into Krivi's computers yet?"

"Not yet. I was considering the best way to go about it when Gutenberg went online."

"We need to know what Krivi is doing," Elizabeth said. "I don't think AEON would release the plague without a vaccine to protect them. If any of the samples survived Zürich, he'll be manufacturing it. That would tell us it's still out there."

"And if it is?"

"We'll deal with that when we get to it."

"I'd like to go through the files I downloaded from Gutenberg before I do anything about Krivi," Stephanie said.

"All right," Elizabeth said. "In the meantime, I'll think about how we're going to deal with Vysotsky."

"Is there some reason why Selena doesn't like the Russians?" Stephanie asked.

"A lot of people don't like the Russians. Why do you ask?"

"It's just that every time we talk about Russia her face shuts down, like she's trying to hide her thoughts or feelings. I didn't think anything of it the first time but then it happened again, more than once. I just wondered if you knew anything about it."

"I can't think of any reason," Elizabeth said. "She was fine working with Korov."

"It's probably nothing," Stephanie said.

CHAPTER 30

The contents of Gutenberg's computer were a
bombshell. Stephanie had just finished briefing
everyone on what she had found and on the contents
of his diary.

"People like him make you wonder if there's
any hope for the human race," Ronnie said. "How
can someone write a business plan for killing
millions of people?"

"It's been done before," Nick said. "You ever
hear of the Wannsee conference?"

"No."

"It was a meeting of high-ranking Nazis, where
they planned the extermination of the Jews. A
business meeting."

Ronnie shook his head.

"I think those names mentioned in Gutenberg's
diary are the people running AEON," Elizabeth
said.

"There's nothing that tells us exactly who they
are," Selena said. "We know about Gutenberg and
Krivi. Why do you think the others are part of
AEON?"

"For one thing, each is wealthy and powerful
and that's a requirement for membership in AEON's
top tier. Take Kamarov, for example. Aside from
the President Gorovsky, Kamarov is possibly the
most powerful man in Russia. Nobody knows his
real wealth. He has his hand in everything. Even the
Russian Mafia stays clear of him."

There it is again, Stephanie thought. *As soon as
Elizabeth mentioned Russia, Selena looked like*

she'd swallowed a lemon. Something's going on there.

Elizabeth continued. "Thorvaldson is probably Aapo Thorvaldson, the shipping magnate. He's in the same money league as Gutenberg and Krivi. De Guillame could be the French Foreign Minister, although that's just an educated guess. Mitchell is a common name but it feels like he might be an American, judging from what Gutenberg wrote."

"Lots of Mitchells out there," Ronnie said.

"How many of them have the kind of money and clout the others carry?" Nick asked.

"I can think of one," Selena said. "Senator Randolph Mitchell. He's rich and powerful and his political philosophy fits right in with AEON's goals."

"I hope you're wrong," Elizabeth said.

"What about the other one, Halifax?"

"I'm not sure," Elizabeth said. "It could be the British Secretary of the Exchequer."

"Oh, that's great," Lamont said. "We're up against three powerful government officials, a Nazi banker, a legal drug lord and two of the wealthiest men in the world. How about a partridge in a pear tree, just for fun?"

"We don't know that Gutenberg is a Nazi," Elizabeth said.

"If it walks like a duck and quacks like a duck..."

Nick said, "Clichés aside, what's our next move? We can't go after these men publicly."

"We have one advantage," Elizabeth said. "They don't know that we know who they are."

"The Russians have the same information we do, if Steph is right," Nick said. "That means they know Kamarov is an enemy of the regime. They might take care of him for us."

"It's possible, but that still leaves the others. We might be able to work with Vysotsky on this. It's just like before, we have a mutual enemy."

"The Russians are our enemy."

Selena's voice was hard and flat. Everyone looked at her.

"The only reason we were able to work with them before was because Korov proved himself our friend and we trusted him. He's dead. We can't trust Vysotsky or any of his people."

"We don't have to trust them," Elizabeth said, "but if the devil himself was useful I'd make an agreement with him to stop Gutenberg and AEON."

Selena sniffed. "Don't say I didn't warn you."

Elizabeth was annoyed. "Let me worry about Vysotsky."

"So what do you want us to do, Director?" Nick said.

"Gutenberg's diary says they're going to release the plague to test it out. Until we know where, all we can do is monitor Gutenberg's computer and hope he reveals the location."

"And when we know it?

"Then you go in and stop them."

CHAPTER 31

The village of Sao Bendito was gripped with fear. Candles burned day and night in the church. There was always someone kneeling and beseeching God to remove the affliction He had sent upon them. If the villagers had known who was really responsible, they would have stopped praying and headed for the clinic with their machetes instead of their rosaries.

The clinic was overwhelmed. Bodies lay everywhere, wherever there was space on the floor, or outside under an improvised shelter. By the time they got to the clinic they were already in the latter stages of the disease. No one lay there for long. A day, perhaps two, spent in the illusion of a possible cure and then they were carried off in a makeshift shroud and buried in a mass grave. Funerals were no longer held at the church. The priest had been an early victim. An ancient backhoe that had been the village pride and joy worked overtime digging pits to bury the bodies.

Karl Schmidt looked out over the chaos and tried not to breathe the stench through the surgical mask hooked over his face. A woman lay coughing and moaning in pain on a makeshift bed on the floor of the clinic. He looked down at her and made a few notes in a small notebook he carried. He knew she would be dead before the day was out.

The woman was nineteen years old and had been beautiful, only a week before. She lay in a pool of urine and blood, a ghastly shell of her former self. Cracked, black blotches that looked like poisonous flowers had spread over her body.

Schmidt's scientific curiosity had gotten the better of him and he'd stayed longer than he'd planned. Besides, he had faith in the vaccine he'd developed. Even so, there was no need to push his luck. Sao Bendito was isolated but it was only a question of time before word got out and the area was quarantined by the government. He'd give it another day and then he was going back to Europe and civilization.

Doctor Silva was away from the clinic, out on the Indian reservation where the plague had already killed hundreds. By the time he returned, Schmidt would be gone.

There was nothing more to do here. He stepped out of the foul-smelling shack and into the clean, humid air of a sub-tropical morning and stripped off his mask. Schmidt took a deep breath and dropped the mask in a trashcan by the door. Somewhere a chorus of monkeys chattered. A flock of brilliantly colored parrots rose from the tops of the trees, the sun lighting up the vibrant red and gold and blue of their feathers. He watched them take flight.

Schmidt took another deep breath and smiled. Yes, it was a beautiful day.

CHAPTER 32

"It's Brazil," Stephanie said. "They released the plague in a village called Sao Bendito. It's in a very remote area."

"How did you find out?" Selena asked.

"Krivi's scientist, Schmidt. He's in charge of the test. He emailed Gutenberg with a progress report and my program captured it. According to the email, everyone who didn't receive the vaccine is dying like flies. Schmidt used a free vaccination program in a clinic as a cover while he infected everyone."

"I screwed up," Nick said. "We didn't get all the samples."

"Don't blame yourself," Elizabeth said. "It figures they'd have them in more than one place in case something went wrong."

"These people need to be put down," Stephanie said.

"That's not like you, Steph."

"If you read that email, you'll feel the same way," Stephanie said. "Schmidt talks about the suffering of these people as if they were lab rats."

"For him, they are," Nick said.

"Do we have any satellite shots of the area?" Elizabeth asked Stephanie.

"We do, but they aren't very good. That area of the world isn't on the list for priority surveillance. I thought you might want to see the photos, so I got them ready."

She touched a key on her laptop. The wall monitor across from Harker's desk came to life with a photograph of a small cluster of buildings in a vast sea of foliage. An unpaved road leading to the town ended in a square in front of the village church. To the north lay a vast area of rivers and grasslands dotted with scattered clusters of huts.

"Zoom in on the town please, Stephanie," Elizabeth said.

"Not much of a town," Lamont said.

"Talk about the Third World," Ronnie said. "That place makes the boonies look like New York City."

"Where's this clinic they're using?" Nick asked.

"I'm not sure," Stephanie said.

Harker pointed at the photograph. "There's activity around that shack on the north edge of town. That might be it. Steph, what's the big open area on the top of the photograph?"

"An Indian reservation, set aside by the government. It's protected."

"Not anymore," Nick said. "Not if they've let that stuff loose. It may be too late to stop them but we can close them down before they do any more damage."

"It makes sense Gutenberg would choose a place like this," Selena said. "It's isolated, hard to get to. Away from prying eyes. My guess would be that the government wouldn't be in a big hurry to do something about illness on that reservation, even if they knew about it. Look at that country, it's perfect ranchland. There must be a lot of people who would like to see the Indians disappear."

"Sounds familiar," Ronnie said.

"I don't think they'd use a house or the church for a clinic," Nick said. "My bet is on that building as the primary target. If we're wrong, it shouldn't take long to find the right one."

"How do you want to go in?" Lamont said.

"We have to shut this down fast. There's only one way to get in there without losing a lot of time."

"Airdrop," Ronnie said.

"I don't see an alternative, but extraction's going to be hard."

"I have a solution for that," Elizabeth said. "The Fourth Fleet is conducting exercises with the USS Carl Vinson off the coast of Guyana as we speak."

"The super carrier?" Lamont said. "That is one mother of a ship."

"That's the one. They have Ospreys on board. That aircraft has enough range to bring you out."

"That would work," Nick said. "How long will it take to set up?"

Elizabeth looked thoughtful. "I have to make a phone call or two but it shouldn't take more than a few hours. In the meantime, you can get everything together."

"What about protective gear?" Selena said. "It's plague. We're going to come across people who have it."

"You won't be treating anyone. As long as you stay away from them you should be all right. The main problem is that this variety is airborne."

"We could use M-50s," Lamont said. "They're rated for everything but the kitchen sink."

"What's an M-50?" Selena asked.

"A biological warfare mask," Nick said. "Lamont's right, it would protect us against anything airborne. It's a full face mask with a good field of view. Plus it's got twin filters that make it easier to breathe and you can put a voice mike on it. Hot, but it keeps you alive. The filters are good for 24 hours. We do this right, we won't be there that long."

"How do we get over the target?" Selena asked.

"Straight from Andrews. I'll send you in a C-130."

"I always wanted to see Brazil," Lamont said.

CHAPTER 33

Ilya Yezhov watched the black Mercedes
bearing Konstantine Kamarov approach the private
airport where Kamarov's Dassault Falcon waited.
Yezhov had dressed like an aircraft maintenance
worker, in baggy white overalls, jacket and cap. He
stood under one of the wings, pretending to inspect
something. A Bizon submachine gun was hidden
under the jacket. The 9mm Bizon was light, reliable
and lethal at close range. It was one of Ilya's
favorite weapons,.

A second member of his team stood on a step
ladder at the rear of the plane, as if he were working
on one of the engines. The pilot and crew were
under guard in the wooden shack that passed for a
terminal. Three men were inside the plane, out of
sight. The cabin door was open and the stairs
lowered to the tarmac. The rest of the strike team
were concealed at strategic points on the perimeter
of the runway. One of Yezhov's snipers was
concealed behind a fuel truck. He carried a .308
Steyr-Mannlicher SSG-08. Ilya thought the Steyr
was the best choice for medium distance targets.
The sniper's job was to take down Kamarov's
bodyguards. A second sniper was positioned with
the heavier .50 caliber Steyr HS50. He would
disable the Mercedes before moving to secondary
targets.

All the others on the team carried the new AN-
94s. Ilya didn't like them. They were over-
engineered, fussy and unreliable in the field, not
like the old Kalashnikovs. Great when they worked,
junk when they didn't. They'd been forced upon him

by the armorer back at the base. He decided to speak to General Vysotsky about it when he got back.

Yezhov dismissed his thoughts about the AN-94. He spoke into his headset.

"Target approaching."

Answering clicks told him everyone was ready. The Mercedes turned off the access road and onto the private airstrip toward the aircraft. It stopped twenty feet away from the foot of the stairway, not far from where Ilya stood. He couldn't see Kamarov through the smoked glass windows but he knew the man was inside. Doors opened on the car and three men got out. They were large men, dressed in dark suits and ties. Ilya knew one of them, a former Spetsnaz corporal who'd been trouble when he was under Ilya's command.

The man saw him. His eyes widened in recognition. Yezhov's cover was blown.

"Go," Yezhov said into his microphone.

The calm atmosphere of the afternoon vanished with the first shot from the Steyr .308. Ilya's former corporal was lifted off his feet and thrown backward as the massive bullet struck his chest. Another shot followed close on the first. The second bodyguard screamed and spun in a bizarre pirhouette before he fell to the pavement. The third man ducked behind the Mercedes but the car suddenly accelerated away from the plane, open doors swaying crazily in the air. It left him exposed. A third shot brought him down.

Yezhov ran after the car, his Bizon out and ready. He shouted into his microphone.

"Take the shot, damn it. Stop that son of a whore before he gets away."

The distinctive boom of the .50 caliber rifle cut through the air. The round tore into the engine compartment of the Mercedes. The car kept moving. A second shot blew through the window on the driver's side. The car slowed and turned left, out of control. Black smoke and oil streamed from underneath. Through the shattered window Yezhov saw the driver slumped to the side, covered with blood. The Mercedes circled back toward the plane and slammed into the nose wheel of the Dassault.

The front of the sleek jet dropped onto the hood, smashing the windshield and pinning the Mercedes underneath. A thin tongue of fire shot out from the engine compartment.

The rear door opened and a fat man wearing a mink coat stumbled out and fell on his knees. Yezhov was on him in an instant.

"Get up, you fat pig." He dragged the oligarch away from the burning car. The flames started to spread to the plane, buried with its nose in the windshield.

Kamarov looked at the muzzle of the Bizon. He licked his lips. "Who are you? Do you know who I am?"

Yezhov slapped him. It was like slapping a side of beef.

"Shut up."

Two Skorpion armored vehicles sped across the runway from their hiding spot behind the terminal building and screeched to a stop next to Yezhov and his captive.

"All units, in," Yezhov said into his microphone.

His men converged on the two trucks. As they moved away, Yezhov looked back and saw the plane beginning to burn. Thick smoke roiled out of the open door and flames lit the interior. The trucks had reached the access road when the gas tanks exploded. A tall column of orange fire erupted into the afternoon, scattering chunks of the expensive jet in every direction.

"My plane," Kamarov said. "You will be sorry for this."

"Let me give you a piece of advice," Yezhov said.

Kamarov looked at him with pure hatred. His eyes were piggy and red, set back in the folds and creases of his dissipated flesh. Ilya caught a glimpse of the ruthless man who was feared by everyone in Russia.

"You have nothing to say of value to me," Kamarov said. "I will have you fed to my dogs." He looked away, out the window

Yezhov took out his knife and drove it into the top of Kamarov's thigh, right to the bone, careful to miss the femoral artery. Kamarov screamed. Ilya withdrew the knife and wiped it on Kamarov's pants.

"Do I have your attention now ?"

"Yes, yes." Kamarov clutched his leg. Dark blood welled up between his fingers.

"My advice to you is this," Ilya said. "You will be questioned. Tell the truth, and you may yet live to think about it. One way or another, we will find out what we want to know. The choice is yours about how painful that questioning may be. Have you heard the value in what I say?"

Yezhov held up the bloody knife. Kamarov looked at him and for the first time showed fear.

"Yes. I have heard you."

Yezhov nodded. "Good."

The rest of the ride was spent in silence, except for Kamarov's moans of pain when the truck hit a patch of rough road.

CHAPTER 34

The mission to Brazil was underway. Stephanie retreated to her computer room and waited for Nick to report in.

She'd been thinking about Selena.

Stephanie's life revolved around her work. She was an introvert, happiest when immersed in the world of her computers. For Stephanie, the powerful Crays at her disposal were more than machines. They were friends, almost human, guides into the infinite layers of secrets hidden away on the computers of allies and enemies.

Stephanie liked to practice her skills by hacking into the files of the world's intelligence agencies. Once she was in, she'd begin looking for information. What exactly she was looking for depended on whether it was related to an assignment or to her personal curiosity.

Today it was curiosity. She was at her console in the computer room, looking for something that might explain Selena's animosity toward the Russians. She felt a little bit guilty about it. It would be easy to misinterpret what she was doing as busybody snooping. It wasn't her intention to snoop, not really. Stephanie was fiercely loyal to Elizabeth and to the Project. She liked Selena a lot, but something was definitely off with her. It might be something that could affect the Project and she was determined to try and find out what it was.

She'd gone through Langley's revolving firewalls and was into the archived records section, searching for anything they might be related to Selena. CIA was certain to have a file on her. Hell, they had reports on everyone connected to the intelligence community. She'd once looked for her own file and was amazed at the details it contained. It had taken her a day or two to get over her indignation, but in the end she couldn't deny that it went with the territory. If you worked for the government, they had a file on you. If you worked in intelligence, that file would be classified and extensive.

Stephanie entered the parameters for her search. Two file references popped up on her screen. She opened the first and skimmed through it. It contained basic health and education history, results of Selena's polygraph tests, evaluations and a record of increasing levels of security clearance. It was standard stuff with nothing unusual. The second file reference led to a section of the archive that was locked away behind a new firewall and the highest security restriction.

Someone went to a lot of trouble to hide this. I wonder why?

After several minutes she was rewarded with the first page of a file about someone called Joseph Connor.

Not Selena, Stephanie thought. She was about to click away when she saw Selena's name midway down the page. She read a few sentences and took a deep breath. She transferred the contents of the file to her own computer, shut down access to Langley and began reading.

A half hour later she sat back in her chair, stunned by what she had discovered.

Joseph Connor was Selena's father. Her father, mother and older brother had died in a car crash when Selena was ten years old. The file revealed that it hadn't been an accident. Joseph Connor had been an agent for the CIA and he'd been murdered by the KGB. Selena's family had been murdered by the Russians.

That wasn't all. The file identified her father as a double agent passing information to Moscow. The file was deliberately vague about whether or not he had been working with the blessings of the seventh floor. The report concluded that he'd been eliminated because the Russians no longer trusted him.

Stephanie sat back in her chair, stunned. *If Selena knows about this, it would explain what I'm seeing in her. But how could she have found out? I wonder if Nick knows anything?*

Stephanie printed out the file and put it in a manila folder. She had to go to Elizabeth with this. She stood and went upstairs. Elizabeth was in her office, leaning back in her chair with her eyes closed.

She looks tired. Stephanie knocked on the open door.

"Got a minute?"

"Come on in, Steph."

"I've got something you need to look at," Stephanie said. "Have you noticed that Selena seems uncomfortable lately whenever something comes up involving the Russians?"

"Now that you mention it, she did seem a little irritable the other day when we were talking about them."

"I think I know why."

Stephanie handed the folder to Elizabeth.

"What's this?"

"Read it and then we can talk about it."

Stephanie sat down as Elizabeth began reading. After a few minutes, Elizabeth looked up and said, "Where did you find this?"

"Buried in the deepest hole Langley could dig, behind half a dozen layers of security."

"Does Selena know about this?"

"I don't know for sure," Stephanie said, "but if she does it would explain why she's so reactive when the subject of Russia comes up."

"She was fine working with Korov."

"She'd come to know and trust him," Stephanie said. "He was like one of the team, for a while there. And if she does know, maybe she found out after he was killed."

Arkady Korov was a Spetsnaz officer who'd worked for General Vysotsky. He'd been seconded to Elizabeth in an unusual alliance between enemies formed out of mutual necessity. He'd been killed in the field while the team was on a mission to stop an unbalanced general from establishing a fascist police state in America.

"How would she find out about this if it was buried?" Elizabeth asked.

"That's a good question. I think we have to ask her."

"You do realize what this could do to her if she isn't already aware of what's in this file."

"I know," Stephanie said.

"Why would Langley hide this away?"

"The file shows that Selena's father was working for the Russians at the same time he was working for us. What it doesn't show is whether or not he was a traitor. The Russians killed him, so they must have thought he'd betrayed them. That would seem to vindicate him."

"Then why not acknowledge him?" Elizabeth said. "Put it in his record. Put one of those anonymous stars up on the wall at Langley."

"It could be a cover-up," Stephanie said. "Maybe someone screwed up and blew his cover. Someone high up. It wouldn't be the first time Langley got an agent killed because someone made a mistake. Or there could have been a mole at the agency. Someone who told the Russians he was a double."

"Not many people would have known what Connor was doing," Elizabeth said. "It would have to be someone with a lot of authority."

"Someone who was high up at the time," Stephanie said.

"The agency had a lot of failures back then. That was when Aldrich Ames was there. He was right in the middle of clandestine ops, he knew who the doubles were. No one really knows how many people he betrayed. He never told them everything after he was arrested."

"But why cover it up? Ames is the most public example of a traitor within the CIA that there is. There wouldn't be any point in hiding something he'd done from an internal point of view."

Elizabeth tapped the file with her pen. "The last entry is dated nineteen eighty-seven. Ames was still there when this was written. Maybe he buried it. He wouldn't want anyone to find out he'd betrayed Connor to the Russians. It wouldn't have been difficult to make it look as though Connor was the mole. The agency knew they were harboring a traitor and they were looking for him. If Ames set Connor up, it would have taken some of the heat off him."

"You think Ames framed Connor?"

"It's possible," Elizabeth said. "Either way, we have to talk to Selena about this."

"What about Nick?" Stephanie asked.

"What about him?"

"If Selena knows about this, it's a good bet Nick does too. I think he should be here when we talk with her."

Elizabeth opened her desk drawer and took out a bottle of aspirin. She washed three tablets down with cold coffee.

"We have to wait until after they get back from Brazil to do it. Steph, can you find out anything else about Connor? The accident? Who was his handler?"

"That's another thing," Stephanie said. "His case officer was William Connor, Selena's uncle."

Elizabeth tried to rub away the headache growing behind her forehead.

"This gets more complicated all the time."

Stephanie said, "DCI Hood was around back then. Do you think he might know something about it?"

"It's possible," Elizabeth said. "I have to think about whether I should approach him about this. Whatever her father did or didn't do, it's nothing to do with her. I don't want her to feel that she's under suspicion because of what's in this file."

"It might be useful to find out who ordered his death," Stephanie said. "Connor was stationed in East Berlin for two years before he was killed. A lot of the Stasi and KGB records from back then were discovered after the wall came down. Finding out more about Connor's death could help us decide if he was a traitor or a patriot. If we can clear him, it would make things a lot easier for Selena."

"All right. We'll talk to her when they get back. That should give you time to find out whatever you can."

"I'm on it," Stephanie said.

Elizabeth looked at the row of clocks on the wall across from her desk.

"They should be over the drop zone just about now."

CHAPTER 35

Helmets, battle dress and MP-5s. Pistols and plenty of ammunition. Ronnie carried a separate pack with C4 and detonators, just in case. Tropical air blew through the open hatch of the C-130. With it came the smell of the Brazilian rain forest rushing by four thousand feet below. Nick waited for the green light that would signal it was time to jump. The voice of the jump master sounded in his headpiece.

"Get ready. Thirty seconds."

Behind Nick, Selena felt the first rush of adrenaline. This was her second jump since she'd joined the Project. The first had been a high altitude jump over the Himalayas from 23,000 feet. This looked like a piece of cake compared to that.

The light turned green. "Go!" Nick said.

He leapt from the plane, counted seconds and pulled his rip cord. The harness grabbed him hard in the groin and pulled as the chute blossomed open. The ground was coming up fast, a cleared field on the border between the rain forest and the Indian reservation. Nick pulled on the steering toggles and guided himself toward what looked like a soft spot. He looked up and saw the others above him.

So far, so good.

The landing zone wasn't as soft as it looked. Pain shot up his spine as he hit, a reminder of the last time he'd done this. He struggled to his feet and pulled the chute in. Five minutes later, everyone was gathered on the edge of the clearing.

"You're limping," Selena said.

"It's nothing." Nick took out a map.

He looked up and scanned the drop zone. "We're right where we wanted to be."

A fast running stream bordered the far edge of the clearing. Beyond, a narrow path disappeared into the trees. He pointed at the path.

"That's where we're going. It will take us close to the clinic. We won't know what we're up against until we've got eyes on it. The people living here have nothing to do with this, so don't assume everyone is hostile. But don't get careless either. It's a safe bet any Europeans you see could be part of Schmidt's group. If you see Schmidt, don't kill him. We want him alive."

"What about the plague?" Selena asked.

"Better put the masks on now. Anyone we meet could be infected. Make sure you're bloused up tight. There could be fleas and fleas carry plague."

Selena bent down and checked that her pants were pulled tight around the tops of her boots.

"If Schmidt's here, he must have heard the plane," Ronnie said. "He'll know something's up."

"He won't know what it is," Nick said. "Anyway there's nothing we can do about it. Let's get the masks on."

They pulled on the masks. Lamont helped Selena adjust the straps until the mask was tight against her face.

"All set." Lamont smiled at her.

"Whatever this is made of, it stinks."

Lamont laughed, the sound muffled behind the mask. "You'll get used to it."

"I feel like the creature from the black lagoon," she said.

"Yeah, you kind of look like it too. You like those old sci-fi movies?"

"I love them. All those tacky rubber creatures. My favorite is *The Attack of the Crab Monsters*."

"Mine's *The Attack of the Giant Tomato*," Lamont said. "It's gotta be the worst movie ever."

"*The Blob*," she said

"*Attack of the 50 Foot Woman.*"

"How about *The Incredible Shrinking Man*?"

"That was cool," Lamont said. "The scene with the spider was really creepy."

"Are you guys about done with the film review?" Nick said.

His words were clear, with an odd mechanical quality caused by the voicemitter and mike on the front of the mask.

"Sorry," Lamont said.

"What's this indicator do?" Selena asked.

"If it turns blue it means the filter is no good anymore," Ronnie said. "We should be out of here long before that happens."

"Weapons hot," Nick said. The safeties on the MP-5s clicked off.

"Everyone ready? Let's go."

They set off along the edge of the trees toward the trail.

CHAPTER 36

Schmidt heard the roar of the plane as it passed overhead and knew it meant trouble. He stepped outside in time to see it disappearing over the trees. It had American markings.

Transport, he thought. *Military. There's no reason for them to be in the area or to be flying low like that. They must be coming here. It's time to leave.*

Schmidt went back inside the clinic building. There had always been a chance someone would discover what was happening and attempt to intervene. Schmidt had anticipated the possibility of government interference, but he hadn't anticipated that it would come from the Americans.

There couldn't be any evidence left behind. He'd been getting ready to leave but he'd thought there would be more time to remove all traces of what he'd done. Now that wasn't possible. Fortunately, he'd prepared an alternative scenario.

Just in case.

The inside of the clinic looked like a medieval painting of hell, dark and full of suffering. Every place where someone could lie down was filled. The floor was covered with victims of the plague. More lay outside in a makeshift, open shed. The room stank of vomit and feces and old blood.

Schmidt picked his way carefully through the dead and dying, ignoring clutching hands and pleas for water. He walked to a tall cabinet next to a sink and opened the doors. The lower part was taken up by a small refrigerator powered by a generator outside the shack. That was where the remaining plague inoculations and vaccine were stored. He took out the glass vials and emptied them into the sink.

The upper part of the cabinet contained supplies on one side and a large, locked wooden box on the other. Schmidt took the box down and opened it. Inside was a steel gray cylinder attached by colored wires to a battery-powered digital timer. The cylinder contained enough explosive to obliterate the shack and everything else in the vicinity.

How long before they get here?

Schmidt set the timer and activated the device. Cries for water followed him as he hurried out of the clinic. He got into his truck and drove away. In two hours he would be out of the country. He never looked back as the dying village disappeared behind him.

A few minutes later, Nick and the others reached the edge of the town where it butted up against the Indian reservation. They'd seen no one on the trail. Nick held up his hand to signal a stop. The shack housing the clinic was fifty yards away, across a field of grass. It was made of wood with a rusted tin roof. Next to the clinic was a hastily constructed open shed of thin poles holding up a thatched roof.

"There are people over there," Selena said.

"Plague casualties," Nick said. His voice was hard. "There must be seventy or eighty people lying there."

"I don't see anyone taking care of them," Lamont said.

"Probably too scared to get near," Ronnie said.

"This is awful." Selena batted away an insect buzzing around her face. "What shall we do?"

"We can't do anything for them," Nick said. "We have to try and find evidence of what caused this and Gutenberg's involvement. We'll go over there. Selena and I will go inside while you two keep watch."

"What if Schmidt's in there?" Ronnie asked.

"I kind of hope he is," Nick said, "but I seriously doubt it. He's probably long gone."

"What are we looking for?" Selena asked.

"Papers, lab equipment, samples of the plague, anything that might point a finger at Gutenberg and Krivi. Schmidt, too. I'll photograph anything we don't want to take with us."

They started across the grass toward the shack. They heard moans and cries from the plague victims as they neared the clinic. The sound sent chills up and down Selena's spine. Some of the people lying outside under the makeshift shelter weren't moving, with the kind of stillness on them that made her think they were dead. In their fever and delirium, many had torn off their clothes. Even this far away, she could see black blotches on the bodies.

"Everyone check your mask," Nick said. "Make sure you're good. All those people are infectious."

"I'm glad we can't smell this," Lamont said.

"It must've been like this when the black death hit Europe," Selena said.

"I saw a movie once that was set in the time of the black death," Nick said. "It was about this knight who traveled around Sweden, playing chess with Death. It was bleak as hell, filled with skeletons and piles of bodies and people whipping themselves. Depressing."

Selena was walking just behind Nick. "I know the one you mean," she said.

Nick reached up to scratch his ear. She was about to say more when the shack disappeared in a violent clap of sound. The shock wave hit her with a blast of heat and wind that knocked her backward onto the ground. Fragments rained down all around. A spear of flying glass drove itself into the ground close to her leg.

Nick climbed to his feet, shaking his head to clear it. Ronnie lay unconscious in the dirt. Lamont was on his knees. Nothing remained of the shack or the shed. A thick column of black smoke rose cloud-like into the sky from a deep crater in the ground.

"Everyone all right?" Nick said. His voice sounded dead, muffled. The blast had shocked his hearing.

Selena was dazed. She looked at the shard of glass sticking out of the ground. It had just missed her.

I could have been killed. If that had cut me, I'd be infected now.

Ronnie sat up and rubbed his forehead. Lamont stood on unsteady legs next to him.

"You two all right?" Nick asked.

"Yeah," Lamont said. "Good thing we weren't any closer." He looked down at his uniform. There were red spatters on it.

"Oh, man, this is blood."

"It's on all of us," Selena said. "It must be from the people in the clinic."

Nick didn't want to think about plague infected blood.

"Lamont, you've got stuff on you," Ronnie said.

A piece of tissue had landed on Lamont's shoulder. He looked at it. It was an eyeball, a squashed human eyeball. He made an odd sound.

"Lamont, don't," Nick yelled. "Keep it down, don't lift your mask."

It was too late. Lamont pulled his mask away from his face and vomited a yellow stream onto the dirt. He lifted his hand toward his lips and stopped as he realized what he was doing. He dropped the mask back down over his face.

Nick used the tip of his knife to brush the eyeball off Lamont's shoulder. He shoved the knife into the dirt and left it there.

"You okay now?"

"Yeah."

"We'll go back and call for extraction. We're not going to find evidence now."

"Nick, we could be infected." Selena's face was pale.

"We're probably all right, " he said. "Unless blood got in an open cut or in your eyes, you should be okay."

He didn't know if that was true or not but it sounded good. Plague wasn't like ebola. At least he hoped it wasn't.

"Get out the medical kits. They were covered up and won't be contaminated. Use antibacterial wipes to clean off your hands and give yourself a shot of antibiotics. They might not help, but it's better than nothing. Make sure you sterilize the area before you do a shot. The first thing we'll do when we get on the ship is head for sick bay. They'll quarantine us until they get test results."

Lamont looked like he might be getting ready to throw up again.

"There's no point in worrying about it," Nick said. "They'll run tests. Come on, we're wasting time."

They went through the ritual of giving themselves shots and started back the way they'd come. Back at the drop zone, Nick opened the comm link to Virginia.

"Director, get us out of here."

Elizabeth could hear the stress in his voice. "What happened?"

"It's a mess. We saw a lot of people who were sick or dead. Schmidt left a bomb that went off and destroyed the clinic. There's nothing left. We won't find any proof of what he did."

"Was anyone hurt?"

"No, but tell the extraction team to bring new BDUs for us. The ones we're wearing have been contaminated. We can't get on a chopper wearing them."

Elizabeth felt her stomach tighten.

"Copy that," she said. "Extraction should be there in half an hour."

"Copy. Out," Nick said.

It was a little more than half an hour before a tilt rotor Osprey with Marine markings settled into the clearing. Three men and a woman wearing nothing but air waited for them. A pile of clothes and equipment smoldered nearby. It was a story that would become legend in the fleet.

CHAPTER 37

Stephanie stretched her arms out to the side and yawned and rubbed her eyes. She'd been searching through the archived files of the East German secret police for more than three hours. Even with the high level translation program she was using, it was tough going wading through the stilted prose of the East German bureaucratic mind. She'd found nothing about Joseph Connor. She decided to give it another half hour before she quit for the day.

Ten minutes later, she got a hit. The first reference led to another and then another, and soon she was looking at the STASI file on Selena's father. The first entry was dated from 1985. Connor had been posing as a businessman interested in taking advantage of cheap East German labor. In the beginning there was only routine surveillance, automatically kept on any western foreigner. About six months after the first entry, everything changed.

Someone in the West had betrayed him. Connor was identified as a high-level CIA agent.

The East Germans decided to compromise him. If they succeeded, Connor would be given the option of cooperation or a bullet. They decided on a classic plan used by every intelligence agency in history. A female operative was assigned to seduce him.

Stephanie's tiredness was forgotten. The file read like a novel written by Frederick Forsyth. But it wasn't a novel. It was the story of a man being drawn into a trap baited with his own weakness.

Stephanie came across the first mention of the KGB. The East Germans knew who their masters were. Because Connor was a potential high level asset, the Russians took over the operation.

Stephanie nodded to herself. She was on the right track, she could feel it.

The KGB chose an experienced agent named Sofia Antipov for the seduction. Antipov was inserted into West Berlin and introduced to Connor by a deep cover East German who was a member of the West German Parliament. Within a month, Selena's father and Antipov were sleeping together. Two months after that, the KGB dropped the hammer.

Joseph Connor was well and truly hooked. He began feeding information back to the Germans and their Russian bosses. It was described in the file as being of significant value. From time to time, deposits of American dollars were transferred into an offshore account in Connor's name. Regular reports were forwarded directly to the chairman of the KGB, Viktor Chebrikov.

That's unusual, Stephanie thought. *Shows how important they thought Connor was. It's beginning to look like he really was a traitor.*

Abruptly, Sofia Antipov was taken out of the picture. Shortly after that, Connor went back to the United States.

I wonder what happened? Stephanie asked herself.

She found out in the next section of the file. Sofia Antipov had gone back to Moscow under a cloud, pregnant with Connor's child. Six months later she'd given birth to a child named Valentina.

Holy shit. Stephanie sat up straight in her chair. *Selena has a half-sister.*

CHAPTER 38

"Are you sure?"

Elizabeth stared at Stephanie.

"I'm sure," Stephanie said. "There are more files to look at but I thought it was best to let you know what I'd already found out."

"How are we going to tell her?" Elizabeth asked. "Should we?"

"I don't know, but she doesn't have any other family. It will be really important to her."

"But her sister is the product of a classic honey trap," Elizabeth said.

"Half sister. I don't think that's the point. What's important is that she's family, even if she is the product of an affair set up by the KGB."

"I wonder why their agent didn't just abort the child?"

"Something else I don't know. There's nothing in the file about that, at least not so far. Maybe she had moral considerations."

"A KGB agent with moral considerations, who behaved like an alley cat in heat?"

Burps the cat was lying nearby. When he heard Elizabeth say *cat*, his ears perked up. He looked at her, yawned, and went back to sleep.

"Burps is listening," Stephanie said. "You should watch your language."

"Very funny, Steph. But this is dynamite. How is Selena going to feel about learning that her father was unfaithful with a Russian spy?"

"You have to tell her what's in this file," Stephanie said.

"I know."

"Selena isn't going to be happy about it."

"Is the sister still alive?"

"I checked. She's alive, all right. There's more. You won't like it."

"More?"

"Not only is she alive, she followed in her mother's footsteps. She works for SVR. Take a look at this."

Stephanie touched a key and a picture of Valentina Antipov appeared on the monitor. It was an official photo from SVR files.

"Good Lord," Elizabeth said. "She looks like a younger version of Selena."

"Take a guess at who her boss and mentor is. I'll give you a hint. His initials are A.V."

"You're kidding," Elizabeth said. "Vysotsky?"

Stephanie nodded. "He's been keeping an eye on her since she was five years old."

Elizabeth reached into her drawer, took out a bottle of aspirin and shook three into her palm. She reached for her coffee cup and washed them down.

"Selena is stubborn," she said. "If she knows the Russians killed her family, she's not going to let it go."

"What if we have to work with the Russians again?" Stephanie asked.

"That could be a problem. Try and find anything that explains why Vysotsky's been so interested in Selena's sister all these years. Look for connections to Selena's father."

Stephanie nodded again. "I'll see what I can do."

Elizabeth looked at her empty coffee cup. "I was about to buzz you when you came in. It didn't go well in Brazil."

"What happened?"

"Schmidt booby-trapped the clinic building and it blew up just as they were approaching. Nick said there was nothing left. They were exposed to infected blood. Right now they're in quarantine on board the carrier. We won't know if they're okay until the ship's medical officer runs tests."

"Elizabeth, that's awful."

"Nick said they saw a lot of people with the plague. They were covered with black blotches and open sores."

"What are you going to do next?"

"I'm going to brief DCI Hood and President Rice and tell them what Nick found," Elizabeth said. "Someone has to tell the Brazilian authorities. That entire part of the country has to be quarantined. It's best if Rice handles it."

"I guess Gutenberg got what he wanted."

"What do you mean, Steph?"

"He proved the plague is effective. Schmidt must have been protected or he wouldn't have been around to set that bomb. They must have a vaccine, which means Gutenberg can move on to the next phase of his plan. I wish we knew what that was."

"I think we're probably going to find out soon enough, " Elizabeth said.

CHAPTER 39

Ilya Yezhov and his sergeant stood a few feet away and looked at the man who liked to think of himself as the most powerful man in Russia. He was naked and sweating. Konstantine Kamarov was clamped immobile into a hard wooden armchair, in a dark room lit only with a single, bright lamp. His huge body bulged out the sides of the uncomfortable chair. The odor of his fear filled the air with a sour, unpleasant scent.

Next to Kamarov's chair was a small metal table on wheels, placed where he could see it. A white towel covered the top of the table. Two rows of polished steel dental and surgical tools gleamed in the light, laid out on the towel in meticulous order. The array of tools was rounded off by a battery-operated electric drill. There was a second chair next to the table. At the moment, it was empty.

They were in an isolated *dacha* on the outskirts of Moscow. It was a place used sometimes when it was important that no one see the prisoner except his interrogators. Curtains covered the windows. The rugs had been removed, revealing a wooden floor scarred with years of use. Dark stains on the wood testified to past interrogations. The dacha had been a favorite of Lavrenti Beria's for questioning special prisoners, when Beria had been head of Stalin's secret police.

The door opened. General Vysotsky and another man entered the room. Vysotsky's companion walked with a limp and wore steel rimmed glasses. His eyes were a watery blue behind the glass lenses. His hair was thinning on top, a nondescript brown color. He had a neat mustache clipped short across his upper lip. The man wore a white laboratory coat. A stethoscope hung around his neck. He carried a small, black bag.

Yezhov recognized him. He didn't know the man's name, but he knew who he was and what he did. The few who knew his occupation called him the Doctor.

Vysotsky walked over to Yezhov. The doctor sat down in the empty chair, opened his bag, and laid out three syringes on the table. He added several vials of liquid and a package of needles. Then he sat back and waited.

Yezhov saluted. "Sir."

"What has he said, Captain?"

"Nothing of value, sir. He did say that he would feed me to his dogs."

"Perhaps he does not understand the seriousness of his situation."

"No sir, I don't believe that he does."

Vysotsky turned to his prisoner. "Do you know who I am?"

"Yes. You are General Vysotsky."

"Do you understand the seriousness of your situation, comrade Kamarov?"

Kamarov's head was clamped to the back of the chair with a steel brace. His eyes darted from side to side. Sweat ran down his forehead. He licked his lips. Vysotsky could see his mind working, searching for a way to turn things to his favor.

"General," Kamarov said. "I can make you a very rich man. Very rich. Wouldn't you like that? Whatever it is you want to know, whatever it is worth to you, I can offer you more."

Vysotsky placed his hands behind his back and looked thoughtful as he considered Kamarov's offer.

"What about my Captain? Would you make him rich also?"

Kamarov smiled.

"Yes, of course. Whatever he desires."

"But you told him you would feed him to your dogs," Vysotsky said.

"I was angry, upset. He'd killed my driver and my guards. I apologize, I didn't mean it."

Vysotsky turned to Yezhov. "You hear that, Captain? He says he's sorry."

"I don't accept his apology."

Vysotsky turned again to Kamarov and sighed. "You heard what he said. I'm afraid that it's out of my hands."

"What do you want?"

"Your friend in Switzerland, Gutenberg. Tell me about him."

"Johannes? What's there to tell? I have business dealings with him, money dealings. He is useful because of his extensive banking connections."

"And your other friends? The Indian who sells drugs, for example?"

"I don't know who you mean," Kamarov said. He licked his lips again.

"Allow me to introduce the man sitting next to you," Vysotsky said.

Kamarov's eyes darted left. Vysotsky continued.

"This is the Doctor. Doctor, this is Konstantine Kamarov. Perhaps you've heard of him?"

"I know who he is." The Doctor's voice was soft and bloodless.

Vysotsky picked up an odd looking surgical tool from the table. He held it in the light and looked at it and showed it to Kamarov.

"What does this do?" he asked the Doctor.

"First I make a few simple cuts across the forehead and around the face. That requires only a scalpel. I lift the scalp and with the tool you have in your hand, I clamp the skin and pull it away. It is then possible to remove the face and hold it up for the subject to see."

Kamarov turned white.

"Is it painful?" Vysotsky asked in a curious tone.

"Oh yes. Then after the subject has seen his face, I hold up a mirror so that he can see what he looks like without it." The doctor's tone was conversational, clinical. "I usually save that procedure for later in the interrogation, if the subject has been uncooperative."

"Can you give comrade Kamarov a brief demonstration of your skills?"

"Certainly."

The doctor drew fluid from one of the vials into a syringe, shot a bit into the air and then injected it into Kamarov's arm. The Russian sucked in his breath.

"It will be a minute or two before it acts," the doctor said. "The drug stimulates the nerve endings and enhances the sensation of pain. Let me demonstrate before it takes effect."

He picked up a scalpel and drew a shallow line along Kamarov's left forearm, leaving a thin trail of blood. Kamarov flinched but said nothing.

"A mere superficial cut," the doctor said, "nothing any of us would consider especially painful."

He looked at his watch. "The drug should be taking effect about now."

He took the scalpel and drew another line on Kamarov's arm, parallel to the first. Kamarov screamed, a sound of agony.

"How long does it last?" Vysotsky asked.

"Usually about two hours. I can keep the subject alive that long. I rarely need to use a second injection." He picked up another tool from the tray. "This one is used to peel skin from other parts of the body."

Kamarov started sobbing. His bladder let go and urine dribbled off the sides of the chair.

"I think he understands the seriousness now," Vysotsky said to Yezhov. "Don't you, Konstantine?"

"Yes, yes. I will tell you what you want to know. Please, get him away from me," he said.

"This is your only chance," Vysotsky said. "Do you understand?"

"Yes, yes, I understand."

"Doctor, please wait in the other room."

"As you wish," the man said, disappointment in his voice. He got up and left the room.

"Tell me about your friend Gutenberg," Vysotsky said again.

Kamarov began talking.

CHAPTER 40

"It was terrible," Selena said. "Those poor people had black...*things*...all over their bodies. Then the building blew up and it rained blood and body parts on us."

It was a Monday morning in Virginia. Through the French doors of Elizabeth's office, Nick saw the cat dozing in the sun on the warm stones of the patio.

"Thank God you weren't infected," Elizabeth said.

"We were buttoned up and lucky," Nick said. "What's happening in Brazil?"

"The government quarantined the entire state of Roraima. There aren't many roads up there and it was relatively easy to isolate. But that doesn't mean the plague won't spread. It's certain the disease got onto the reservation. If they want to, the Indians can travel without being seen. They can go wherever they want and the government can't stop them. So far not much has been done except for the quarantine. Brazil isn't equipped for something like this."

"Have they requested aid?" Selena asked.

"They're playing it down. They don't want to scare off the tourists."

"Reminds me of *Jaws*," Lamont said. "Come on in, the water's fine and there ain't no sharks out there."

"It's not our concern anymore. The question is, what is AEON planning next?"

"Maybe Gutenberg will send out another email that tells us what he's up to," Nick said.

"We can't count on that."

Elizabeth glanced out the window. Burps was awake, eyeing an unreachable bird perched on the roof. His tail twitched in frustration.

"Steph, has there been any unusual activity from Gutenberg?"

"Not really. Although there is one thing that's odd."

Elizabeth raised her eyebrows and waited.

"He's been trying to contact the Russian, Kamarov. There's been no reply. I can tell that he's getting annoyed."

"SVR installed a bug on Gutenberg's computer. That means Vysotsky knows AEON was behind the raid in Russia and that Kamarov was involved. He'll want to interrogate him. That could explain why Kamarov isn't answering Gutenberg's emails."

"You think Vysotsky arrested Kamarov?" Nick asked.

"It's what I'd do," Elizabeth said. "Perhaps not an official arrest. Kamarov's nephew is Vysotsky's boss. He has to be careful. If I were him, I'd grab Kamarov in secret and take him someplace where I could take my time questioning him."

"I might be able to find out where Kamarov is," Stephanie said, "or at least where he isn't. That might tell us something."

Elizabeth nodded. She looked around. "Anyone have anything else?"

No one did.

"Then that's all for the moment. Nick, Selena, please stay for a few minutes. There's something I want to talk with you about."

Ronnie, Stephanie and Lamont left the room. Elizabeth opened a drawer and took out the file on

Selena's father. She opened it to the first page and turned it so that Selena and Nick could see it.

Selena drew in a breath when she saw her father's name.

"Selena, do you know what this is?"

"It's a CIA file about my father."

"Have you seen it before?"

"Shit," Nick said.

Elizabeth waited.

"Yes, I've seen it. I thought it had been destroyed."

"You knew about this, Nick?"

"I knew about it. We didn't tell you because we weren't sure how you'd react. Finding out that Selena's father might have been a Russian spy wasn't exactly a great item for her resume. We were afraid you'd think she was a security risk."

"I don't know what's more disappointing," Elizabeth said. "The fact that you didn't trust me or that you thought I would judge Selena by who her father was."

"He wasn't a traitor." Selena's face was flushed.

Nick said nothing.

"How did you get the file?" Elizabeth asked.

"Adam gave it to me," Nick said. "He said it was the only copy."

"You seemed angry every time Russia came up in our meetings," Elizabeth said to Selena. "Stephanie wondered why. She went looking for reasons why you might be upset. She found this file in a restricted archive at Langley, buried behind a half dozen layers of added encryption."

"Spying on me," Selena said.

"I don't want to hear that," Elizabeth said. "I know that's not what it was and so should you."

"How would you feel? The KGB killed my father, my mother and my brother. I have every right to be angry with the Russians."

"How long have you known?"

"I've known for months."

"You knew about Valentina?"

"Valentina?" Selena said. "Who's Valentina?"

Elizabeth looked at her, surprised. "I think you'd better tell me about the file Adam gave you. What did it say?"

"It was a classified file, obviously old, clearly authentic."

"An actual paper file?"

"Yes."

"Go on."

"It said he was an agent, something I didn't know about him. It said he'd been giving information to the Russians. It listed deposits in his name, hidden in accounts located offshore. There were photographs of him in East and West Berlin, meeting with people identified as Russian agents. There were a lot of details. It said that his death wasn't an accident and that the KGB executed him. The last part concluded that the Russians acted because they no longer trusted him."

"And that was it? Nothing more?"

"The only other thing I discovered was that my uncle also worked for the CIA. I didn't know that, either. His signature was on many of the papers in the file."

Elizabeth sighed. "I can only imagine how you must've felt when you read that."

"No you can't," Selena snapped. She took a breath. "I'm sorry. Yes, it was upsetting. I thought I knew who he was. That got turned upside down."

"There was no mention in the file of any one named Valentina? Or Antipov?"

"No."

"What you getting at, Director?" Nick asked.

"There's more to the story, another section of this file that you haven't seen. Selena, the rest of it is going to come as something of a shock to you."

"I don't think there could be much about this that would shock me after finding out my father was a spy."

"I just wanted to prepare you," Elizabeth said. She pushed the file across her desk. "Read it, and then we'll talk."

Selena took the file and began reading.

CHAPTER 41

The fresh green of approaching spring dusted
the manicured garden beds of the Bois de Boulogne.
Valentina Antipov loved the park, though she
thought that calling the Bois de Boulogne a park
was like calling the Mona Lisa a pretty picture. She
ran here early in the morning every day, unless
prevented by her assignment to Gutenberg. The
spacious grounds in the west of Paris were a
reminder that life was about more than the
unpleasant necessities of her job.

Valentina only vaguely remembered a time
before she'd begun training to be a spy. It had
started when she was five years old, when her
mother took her to a gray building on the outskirts
of Moscow and left her in the care of a man wearing
the uniform of a captain in the KGB. Captain
Vysotsky became the substitute for a father she had
never known. A stern father, a demanding father,
but a father who was stern and demanding was
better than none at all. She saw her mother
infrequently, sometimes not for a months. When
Valentina asked about her, Vysotsky would say that
her mother was a hero and was serving the needs of
the Motherland.

"You can see how important it is, can't you,
Valentina? Your mother works to keep us all safe
and protect us from our enemies. That's why she
can't be here as much as you'd like."

"It's good that she's a hero," Valentina had said,
"but I wish she could spend more time with me."

Valentina had been nine at the time. The
memory was burned into her mind. A day later (or
was it two or three, she couldn't quite remember),

Captain Vysotsky told her that her mother was dead, killed in the line of duty by the treacherous agents of the West.

Years later Valentina found out that the truth was somewhat different. Sofia Antipov had gotten drunk and lost control of her car on an icy mountain road in the Swiss Alps. The car had smashed through the guard rail and plunged over a thousand feet until it shattered on the unforgiving boulders far below.

Valentina's intelligence and motor skills were well above average, a fact that did not escape her teachers' attention. When she reached the age of fourteen she was singled out for specialized training in the art of killing. By the time she was twenty-two, she was expert in all the tools of her trade. Along with martial arts, knowledge of poisons and use of the garrotte, Valentina was gifted with skill in weapons from the present and the past. She could use a Zulu spear or a samurai katana as easily as a Makarov pistol.

A little more than twenty years after her mother's death, Vysotsky had risen to the rank of general and Valentina had been molded into a perfect killing machine.

Morning sun lit the magnificent pavillion of Napoleon III as she ran past. The last French Emperor would have been shocked to see that his pavilion had been converted to a hotel and restaurant. She kept running until she came to the end of the Grand Cascade at the *Lac Inferieur*, the largest lake in the park. Water ran everywhere in the Bois, flowing through artful channels into lakes and ponds and fountains. Valentina slowed her pace to a jog and then to a walk. She found an empty bench facing the lake and sat, letting her body cool. She thought about what the day would bring. She had to meet with her handler later, at a bistro in Montmarte.

Lucien is getting pushy, she thought.

She watched a pair of joggers go by on the path.

Why has he called for another meeting? It's bad tradecraft. I don't like the way he undresses me with his eyes. Lots of men do that and I don't mind, but with him it's different.

For a moment she entertained the thought of placing something unpleasant in Lucien's espresso and watching him die. But of course she couldn't do that unless it became necessary. Lucien was getting careless. She decided to let Alexei know about it.

Alexei Vysotsky was the closest thing to a father that Valentina had ever known. She wasn't sure how to describe her feelings for him. It was probably love, although Valentina wasn't certain what love actually was. Whatever it was, her feeling for Vysotsky was mixed with deep resentment and grudging admiration for the unrelenting discipline he had imposed upon her over the years.

Valentina was proud of her skills. She knew she was one of the stars in Vysotsky's elite group of high level agents. It was unusual for her to be asked to seduce someone and maintain a relationship with them. There were plenty of agents available for that, men and women both, depending on the sexual preference of the target. Her primary role was as an assassin. The fact that Vysotsky had assigned her to Gutenberg told her that sooner or later she'd be ordered to eliminate him.

She hoped it was sooner. Gutenberg was becoming tiresome. Besides, he was a lousy lover. Lucien, on the other hand, was probably quite adept in bed, but Valentina would sooner sleep with a snake than with him.

She rose and started back for her apartment at an easy walk. There was time to go home, shower and change before her meeting. As she walked she was aware of everything in her environment, her paranoia high. That man with an umbrella could as easily be her counterpart from an enemy agency. The woman with a baby carriage might have a gun under those blankets.

Even though Valentina knew that the man with the umbrella was probably anticipating a spring shower or that the baby carriage contained nothing more menacing than a sleeping infant, she remained alert. She was still alive because she never dropped her vigilance.

It was a condition of her occupation.

She passed a couple strolling with their two children. The woman was laughing. She looked happy. The man said something and smiled.

I wonder what it would be like to have a family.

CHAPTER 42

Selena sat in shock, staring at the file in her hands. Elizabeth waited, watching her.

After a long pause, Selena said, "You're sure this is authentic?"

"Yes," Elizabeth said.

"I have a sister who is a Russian agent, an assassin?"

"Half sister. Yes. She works for General Vysotsky."

Nick had enough sense to keep silent.

"I don't believe this. I can't believe it."

"I'm sorry, Selena," Elizabeth said. "I wish it weren't true."

"How could he? How could my father sleep with a Russian whore?"

"It's an old trick," Elizabeth said. "The KGB used sex to compromise a target all the time. Moscow Center was better than anyone at exploiting human weakness. It would have taken a saint to resist. Your father didn't know she was a Russian agent until it was too late. Remember, he was assigned to West Berlin. Every time he crossed into East Germany he risked his life. He would have been threatened with arrest and execution. It doesn't excuse him, but you can understand how much pressure he was under."

"You're right, it doesn't excuse him."

"If you read the file carefully, you'll see that there's no conclusion your father betrayed his country."

"What about the meetings with Russian agents? What about the bank accounts?"

"On the surface that looks bad," Elizabeth said. "But all of it could easily have been part of his assignment. Why would the Russians kill him if they thought he was giving them good intelligence? It's much more likely they discovered he was reporting back to Langley. There were people on the seventh floor who knew what was going on. One of them was Aldrich Ames. He sold out a lot of our agents before he was caught. Your father may have been one of them."

"Then why doesn't it say so in the file?" Selena asked.

"The file was closed in nineteen eighty-seven," Elizabeth said. "Ames was still there. He would have seen it as an opportunity to deflect suspicion away from him."

"We'll never know, will we?" Selena said. There was bitterness in her voice.

"I'd like to talk with Hood about this," Elizabeth said. "He was there at the same time as your father and Ames. He might know something that would cast a little more light."

"It would make a difference to know that he wasn't a traitor. Nothing will change the fact that he cheated on my mother."

"No."

"This woman, Valentina. Where is she now?"

This woman, not my sister, Elizabeth thought.

"I don't know. All we know is that she works under Vysotsky. Stephanie will try and find out more."

Selena stood and dropped the file on Harker's desk. She walked out. They heard the door to the downstairs level slam behind her.

"She's pissed," Nick said.

"Your powers of observation are astounding," Elizabeth said. "I never would have guessed."

"Why did you tell her about her sister?"

"I thought about it and I decided it's too important for Selena. Even if it wounds her to learn that her father was unfaithful, now she knows she has some family left in the world."

"A Russian assassin," Nick said.

"Yes, but still family. She deserved to know."

"I don't think Selena is looking forward to the family reunion."

"It's unlikely that they'll ever meet," Elizabeth said.

"You don't know Selena like I do, Director. Don't count on it," Nick said. He got up off the couch. "I'd better go see how she's doing."

He went down the spiral staircase to the lower level and heard pistol fire coming from the range. Selena stood at one of the stations, bent forward, pistol straight out in front of her, firing at a man sized target fifty feet away.

Ronnie had worked on her Sig 229 to lighten the trigger pull. He'd brought the pull down from four plus pounds to just a touch under three. It made rapid fire easier. Nick watched Selena empty a twelve round magazine in seconds. She wasn't trying for a perfect score, she was shooting for combat accuracy. All except one of the twelve rounds were somewhere in the silhouette's upper body. Most were clustered near the center of the chest.

The slide locked back on her pistol. Selena ejected the empty magazine and laid the gun down in front of her. She saw Nick and took off her shooting glasses and ear protectors.

"He's dead," Nick said. "Nice shooting."

"What am I going to do, Nick?"

"About what?"

"You know what. My father's bastard. My sister."

"I don't know if bastard is quite the right word," Nick said.

"Don't try to make me feel better with your bullshit humor."

"You're right, I'm sorry. It's an old habit when I'm not sure what to say."

"Then don't say anything."

Selena went over to a bench by the wall and sat down. Nick sat beside her.

She looked out the floor. "I thought I didn't have any family left after uncle William died. Now I find out I have a half sister who's a Russian assassin. How the hell do I deal with that?"

"I don't know. I guess it depends on what it means to you. Finding out that you have a sister."

"I want to hate her, but I can't. It's not her fault my father couldn't keep it in his pants."

"You heard what Harker said. Your father was only human. Everybody's got a weak spot and the KGB was really good at setting people up."

"He should have resisted."

"Yeah, but he didn't."

"I wonder if my mother knew that he had an affair."

"I doubt it," Nick said. "Your father was good at concealing what he did and who he was."

"She must've known he worked for the agency."

"She probably did but that would've been about all she knew. He wouldn't have talked about his work."

"What am I going to do?" Selena said again. "I want to know more about her but I can't very well call her up and introduce myself. It's not like she's working in a regular job somewhere."

Nick draped his arm around her shoulders.

"It's complicated, isn't it? Stephanie will find out whatever she can. I think you have to be careful here."

"What do you mean?"

"I'm probably not the best person to talk to about this," Nick said. "My father was a drunk, my mother allowed herself to be abused and my sister is a bitch. I don't have fond memories of family."

"What's your point?"

"Just because she's your half-sister doesn't mean she's family. She's a stranger and she's an enemy. People usually define family by blood ties but I don't see it that way. I think family are the people you can rely on, the people you know who will back you up when you need it. People who can rely on you."

"She's still my sister."

"Yes, she is, but she doesn't know that."

"It could make a difference if she did," Selena said.

"It could. Meanwhile I've got an idea."

Selena looked at him. "What?"

"Let's go get one of those Long Island iced teas you like."

CHAPTER 43

The George V in the heart of Paris had been a favorite hotel of the rich for decades. It was where Gutenberg always stayed when he was in town. He was getting dressed in his room when his encrypted phone signaled a call from Appo Thorvaldson, one of AEON's seven directors.

"Appo. How are you?"

"I'm fine, Johannes, but I'm afraid you are not."

"What do you mean?"

"We have a security breach. Your emails are being intercepted by an outside party."

"What? That's impossible."

"I have a man working for me who takes care of all my electronic security. He monitors everything that comes into my computer. He discovered an anomaly in your last email."

Gutenberg looked at his watch. He was meeting Valentina for dinner.

"Go on."

"Someone has put a tracking program on your computer that allows them to monitor all of your communications."

"You're certain."

"Of course, or I wouldn't bother you."

"How would this be done?" Gutenberg asked. "How could someone get through my firewalls and plant their program?"

"Our security protocols make it unlikely it was done over the Internet. It had to be done by someone with direct access to your computer."

Gutenberg flushed with anger. He kept his laptop with him at all times. There was only one other person who could have gotten to it.

Valentina. She has betrayed me.

"We have to deal with this, Johannes."

"Don't worry, I'll take care of it. I think I know who is responsible. Where are the messages going?"

"We don't know yet. If you send me a long message, we'll have time to trace the signal back to whoever is spying on you."

"Perhaps we can turn this to our advantage," Gutenberg said.

"In what way, Johannes?"

"They don't know we've discovered them. Let me think about it."

"When will you send the message?"

"Tomorrow morning. I'll alert you when I'm ready to do it. And now, I'm going to be late for a dinner engagement."

"Ah, yes, the lovely Valentina. You are fortunate to have such a beautiful mistress."

"I've been growing tired of her. I think it may be time for a change."

"Oh? Do you think she might consider a new liaison?"

"With you?"

"Why not? I don't mind slightly used goods."

Gutenberg thought about what he was going to do when he talked to Valentina about the computer.

"I don't think you'll want to pursue that, my friend."

He ended the call.

In a room three doors down, an SVR technician had been listening to the conversation. He turned off the recorder and took off his headphones. Gutenberg had made a mistake common to men who thought they were invulnerable, the mistake of predictability. He always stayed at the George V when he was in Paris. It had been a simple matter to determine when he would arrive at the hotel and equally simple to put listening devices in his rooms.

The program installed on Gutenberg's computer had been discovered. The technician called the number he'd been given in case there was a problem. Across town, Valentina's handler picked up his phone.

CHAPTER 44

Valentina was getting ready to leave her apartment to meet Gutenberg at the restaurant when her phone buzzed. She looked at the display. It was a text from Lucien, her handler.

She felt a wave of adrenaline ripple through her body. It was a prearranged emergency abort code. She was compromised, in immediate danger. It meant she had to run.

Now.

She'd dressed in high heels and a designer evening outfit from Dior for the evening. It wasn't the best outfit for going to ground. She swore under her breath, kicked off the shoes and dropped the clothes to the floor. She ran to the closet and pulled on black jeans, a shirt and a pair of boots. On the shelf was a leather belt pack with money, passports and a Glock G27. She clipped the pack onto her belt.

Valentina checked the Glock to make sure there was a round in the chamber. The pistol had the advantage of being small and light, with nothing projecting to snag the weapon in a pocket or a purse at an inconvenient time. Nine rounds of .40 caliber hollow points were more than enough. If she needed more, she'd be in trouble.

She pulled on a warm jacket and cracked open the door, the Glock in her right hand. It had been less than five minutes since Lucien had called. The hallway was clear. Valentina let her training take over.

You can't go out the front of the building. They'll have that covered. Same for the back.

She headed for the roof. One of the reasons she'd picked this building was for easy access to the roof. A door at the end of the hall led to a stairwell. She opened it and stepped through. She held the heavy door so it wouldn't slam and shut it behind her.

The building was nine stories tall and her apartment was on the fifth floor. The stairs were brightly lit. She climbed with the easy movements of a predator, her footsteps barely sounding in the hollow space. A door slammed somewhere below. The echo vibrated up through the stairwell. Rapid footsteps sounded on the stairs, coming toward her. It sounded like two men.

Valentina reached the door leading onto the flat roof and went through. Gravel crunched under her feet. Overhead, the Paris sky was without stars. The brilliant glow from the city's millions of lights reflected from a canopy of low hanging clouds. There was a smell of April rain in the air.

The next building over was eight stories high, separated from hers by a narrow alley. It was an easy leap across the gap to the roof on the other side. From there she'd make her escape.

The footsteps coming up the stairs were close. *They'll be here before I can make the jump,* she thought. *If I make it before they get here, I'll be a target. Even if I get away, they'll know where I've gone.*

She pocketed the Glock. Shots would only bring the police.

Valentina's voluptuous looks were deceiving. Her curves hid layers of powerful muscles. She stood to the side of the shed and waited. The footsteps paused, then gravel crunched as someone stepped onto the roof. She slammed the open door into the unseen figure with all her strength. The man cried out in pain.

Valentina came around the door like one of hell's dark angels. She let go with a vicious kick of her steel-toed boot into the fallen man's head. She felt the bones of his face shatter. He screamed. His partner raised a pistol and fired. The shot burned across her upper arm as she drove her stiffened fingers into his throat. He fell backward and rolled down the steps. The body came to rest on the next landing.

Blood ran warm down her arm but there was no time to treat the wound. Valentina turned and ran across the roof and leapt for the top of the building next door. She rolled as she hit, her jaw clamped tight against the pain of her injured arm. She came up moving and ran to the door leading into the building.

The distinctive two-tone wail of a French police car sounded in the distance, coming her way. A second siren joined the first.

Someone heard the shot, she thought.

Valentina had the door open in seconds. She went down the stairs two steps at a time. She reached the ground floor, followed the hall to the back service entrance and disappeared into the Parisian night.

CHAPTER 45

The day after the fiasco with Valentina, Gutenberg was back in his château. He had Krivi on the secure line. They were talking about Brazil.

"The test has gone even better than we hoped," Krivi said. "Schmidt is quite pleased. The plague is spreading nicely. Brasilia has managed to confine the outbreak to the far North for the moment, but people will continue to die. The vaccine has proven effective. My laboratories are ready for production."

"When do you plan to announce the discovery?"

"Later today. There will be delays while the bureaucrats clamor for further testing and safety evaluations for human use. I anticipate that regulations will delay distribution in volume for at least six months."

"Excellent," Gutenberg said.

"How is our stockpile of the plague agent?"

"We have more than enough," Gutenberg said. "It will make the plagues of history pale in comparison."

"Have you heard from Kamarov?" Krivi asked.

"I was about to ask you the same thing. No, I haven't. I'm beginning to think something has happened to him."

"He has many enemies," Krivi said. "I'm surprised he's lasted this long."

"He has excellent security and government protection."

"Even the best security can fail against a determined opponent." Krivi paused. "You didn't call me just for an update."

"You know me too well, old friend. We have a problem. Valentina has betrayed me."

"Ah. For a younger man? I thought you were above that sort of thing."

"Another man in her bed would mean little," Gutenberg said, "though I do expect exclusivity from my mistresses. This is worse than that. She's been spying on me. Someone else is now aware of our plans."

"Thorvaldson told me your emails had been compromised," Krivi said. "That certainly is a problem. What have you done with her?"

"Somehow she knew I'd found her out. I sent men as soon as I discovered her treachery but she killed them. She's escaped."

"Killed them? The lovely Valentina? I never would have guessed she had such skills."

"She installed a program on my computer to monitor my correspondence. She's working for someone with sophisticated resources."

"One of your competitors?"

"No. Valentina was well-trained, she was armed and she was ready to kill in order to escape. She has to be working for a government. Whoever it is knows who we are. That means they are a serious threat."

"The others will be upset by this development," Krivi said. "Mitchell has expressed doubts to me about your leadership. He may try to use this to remove you."

"You didn't tell me Mitchell had approached you."

"I did not feel it was necessary. My sense was that he was exploring possibilities, sounding me out as a possible ally. I left him with the impression that

I was open to persuasion. Personally, I think he's an ass."

Gutenberg laughed. "The fact that the Americans elect people like him to run their country never ceases to amaze me."

"He is very convincing in front of the cameras," Krivi said. "I could almost believe he was telling the truth if I didn't know better."

"An accomplished politician," Gutenberg said. "He may be an ass but he has been effective at furthering our goals. We don't have to like him."

"It is very easy for me not to like him."

"In any event, this spying cannot be tolerated."

"I have asked my man to find out who is listening in," Krivi said. "He said it will take a little time."

"But he can do it."

"Yes," Krivi said.

"Good."

"Perhaps we could draw them out."

"What do you mean?" Gutenberg asked.

"Because of your ex mistress they know we released the plague in Brazil. That makes us a threat to them. If I were them, I would want to remove that threat."

"You think they'll come after us."

"It's possible. They could target us individually but I have a better idea."

"Go on."

"Send me an email discussing our next face-to-face meeting as a group. They will be certain to intercept it."

"We have no such meeting scheduled," Gutenberg said.

"Whoever is monitoring you doesn't know that. If they think we are all going to be together and accessible it will make a tempting target. I thought your place in France might seem believable."

"You think they'll send in a team? Try to assassinate us?"

"Wouldn't you?" Krivi said.

"It's worth a try," Gutenberg said. His voice hissed with suppressed anger. "They are going to regret interfering."

"Have you chosen the target for the next phase?" Krivi asked.

"Let's wait until we find out who has been spying on us. Releasing the plague on their home ground would be fitting punishment for their arrogance."

CHAPTER 46

It was spring outside Elizabeth's office
windows. The lawns at Project headquarters were
turning green. The flowerbeds bloomed with new
life and color. It was a beautiful day, the kind of day
for leaving your desk and sitting somewhere in the
sunshine. For Elizabeth, a day like that was right up
there with one of Samuel Coleridge's opium
dreams. The team was assembled in her office.

"We have a new mission," Elizabeth said.
"Steph?"

Stephanie wore a light blue shirt that hung
loose over black slacks. Elizabeth thought she might
be putting on a little weight, but her clothes hid it
well. As she often did, she'd chosen large gold
earrings. A half dozen gold bracelets circled her left
wrist. Her fingernails were painted a shade of blood
red that matched her lipstick.

"Gutenberg sent a long email to Krivi Dass.
He's called a face-to-face meeting of AEON's
leaders."

"Where?" Nick asked.

"A villa in Normandy, near Caen. Gutenberg
owns a boutique vineyard there. It produces only a
few hundred bottles a year. Very high-end."

"What do you have in mind?" Nick said.

"It's time we ended this," Elizabeth said. "I
want you to go to that villa and put AEON out of
business, once and for all."

"You want us to kill them?" Selena said. "I
thought we were the good guys."

"And they're the bad guys," Nick said. "They've started wars that caused the deaths of millions of people. They killed Adam. Those people we saw dying in Brazil, that's their doing. They gave up any rights to fair treatment a long time ago."

"I didn't say kill them." Elizabeth looked at Selena. "You can try and take them alive. We need to know where the rest of those plague samples are. We need to know what else they've planned, who they've corrupted."

"Director, you really think we can take them alive?" Ronnie asked.

Harker shrugged. "As I said, you can try. There are no rules of engagement if they resist."

Selena's expression showed her disapproval but she said nothing.

"These are important men, public figures," Nick said. "You know they'll resist. People are going to ask a lot of questions if they disappear. They'll have trained pros for bodyguards, probably ex special forces. We go after them at that villa, it's going to get noisy, fast. If we kill any of them, half the police forces in the world will be after us."

"Then you better hadn't get caught," Elizabeth said. "This one is completely off the books. No backup, no extraction. The president will not know about this mission. For this one you don't exist."

"It's not like it's the first time," Lamont muttered.

"I don't think you need to worry about noise," Stephanie said. "I searched through our satellite archives and found pictures of the villa. It's isolated. The house is surrounded by thick hedges on three sides. You could set off a bomb in there and no one would hear it."

"Inside, maybe," Nick said. "Sound carries a long way in the country. Let's see the pictures."

Stephanie clicked her mouse and a satellite photograph of the villa and grounds appeared on the wall monitor. The house was large with a slate roof. A high stone wall with a gate ran across the front of the property along the main road. A long, white gravel drive led straight and flat from the road to the house. Behind the house was a field with rows of grapevines laid out in a neat grid. There were several outbuildings scattered around the villa and another, larger building in back. A tractor was parked next to it.

"What's that building in the back?" Nick asked.

"It's where they crush the grapes," Stephanie said. "You can see an access road from the vineyard that goes right to it."

"The little old winemaker," Lamont said. "Makes me glad I drink beer, if guys like Gutenberg are the ones who make the wine."

"Pretty easy to figure out you drink beer," Ronnie said. "You really gotta work on that gut you're getting."

Harker cleared her throat, loudly. "Focus, please."

"We'll need the jet," Nick said. "Diplomatic papers to get our gear through customs. We can fly into Caen and drive from there. Steph, can you get us a floor plan?"

"I'll search the city archives at Caen. There might be something there. "

"It's not a good idea to go in there blind. That's a big house. It's going to have a lot of rooms."

"I'll task infrared surveillance on the villa," Elizabeth said. "It will tell us how many people are inside and where they are. The Pentagon has upgraded most of the satellite cameras with new technology. It almost makes the roof and walls invisible."

Nick nodded his head. "That will help a lot."

"What are we taking?" Ronnie asked.

"It's a straightforward mission, in and out. The usual stuff. Vests, MP-5s, with silencers. Flash bangs, night vision gear. Comm gear."

"C4?"

"No, but take grenades."

"Frags or offensive?"

"Both."

"Aren't all grenades offensive?" Selena asked. "I mean, it's not exactly a defensive weapon."

"Those are two different types," Ronnie said. "Frag grenades send shrapnel everywhere. Offensive grenades are small bombs with a five second fuse. They're good inside a bunker or a building."

"How do you tell them apart?"

"You're familiar with the frag type. The offensive grenades look like a shaving cream can. They're marked so you know what they are."

"Oh, that's helpful," Selena said.

CHAPTER 47

In Moscow, late snow had buried the promise of spring. No one was surprised. It was always too cold or too hot in Moscow, too wet or too dry. The one thing you could count on was that whatever kind of day it was could change at any moment.

That was as true for Alexei Vysotsky as it was for the weather.

Vysotsky stood at parade rest in front of the desk of the Director of SVR, Boris Vishinski. Vishinski sat in a brown, high back leather chair, studying Vysotsky's report on the interrogation of Konstantine Kamarov. Vishinski had total control of the largest intelligence network in the world. It made him the most dangerous man in Russia.

Standing behind Vishinski was a tall, hawk faced man in civilian clothes. General Kiril Golovkin was head of the GRU, Russian Military Intelligence. Vysotsky had worked with him often and knew him well. He was intelligent and ruthless, a nationalist and a patriot. He wore a patch over his left eye, a gift of the Chechen separatists.

Vysotsky had taken a chance coming here. If Vishinski was part of the plot, Alexei knew he'd be dead by nightfall.

"Where is Kamarov now, General?"

"In a private medical facility where no one will find him," Vysotsky said. "I thought it best to keep him alive for trial and further interrogation."

Vishinski nodded. "Your report says his nephew arranged the attack on the train and the assassination of your men. Have you arrested him?"

"No, sir. That is for you to decide. Without his uncle to give him directions, I feel he can do little damage. I thought he should be left in place until you decide what to do."

"What do you think we should do?" Golovkin asked.

Vysotsky didn't hesitate. "He is a traitor to the motherland. He should be interrogated and shot."

"Sometimes you are so very old-school," Vishinski said. "It's one of the things I appreciate about you, General. In this case you are absolutely right."

Vysotsky felt himself relax, just a little.

"Stand at ease, General. You are making me nervous."

"Sir." He allowed himself to stand easy.

"You have displayed considerable initiative in this matter. It must have been rather confrontational for you, no?"

"Sir?"

"I'm talking about risk. You took a great personal risk in going after Kamarov like that. Why did you do it?"

"Konstantine Kamarov is a pig, feeding on the spoils of our nation. If I'd tried to go through channels and accused him, he would have made sure the accusation turned back on me. I'd be pictured as someone angling for his nephew's job, someone jealous of Kamarov's success and wealth."

"That thought had occurred to me as I was reading your report," Vishinski said. "I understand your caution. But it still does not explain your actions."

"He is responsible for the deaths of my men. That alone would be reason enough for me. He's a traitor. He had to be brought down, one way or another."

Golovkin nodded once, in agreement.

"Take a team and arrest Vladimir Kamarov immediately," Vishinski said. "As of now, you are the new deputy director."

"Thank you, sir."

"You will retain command of Zaslon."

"Sir."

"Put together a plan for elimination of this group, AEON. Subject to my approval, you will put it into effect," Vishinsky said. "I will want daily progress reports but nothing in writing. Make sure nothing leads back to us. The names in this report are too important. The British Chancellor of the Exchequer and the French Foreign Minister, for starters. It's unbelievable. There's even a U.S. Senator."

"It explains a lot, doesn't it?" Vysotsky said.

"How do you mean?"

"The sanctions, the propaganda, the false accusations of atrocities while they secretly create crisis after crisis. All designed to turn world opinion against us. These men in AEON have been manipulating events for years. They are driving us to war."

"All the more reason we must stop them," Golovkin said.

"The world will be destroyed if there is war," Vysotsky said.

"Yes," Vishinski said. "So you had better get to work."

CHAPTER 48

The mission was a go.

They landed in France in the late afternoon. Their diplomatic papers took them through customs without trouble or an inspection that would have turned up the arsenal they'd brought with them. They rented a nondescript van and loaded an aluminum trunk holding their gear into the back. Gutenberg's wine country retreat was about an hour from the Caen airport. Selena drove. Her fluent French would smooth things if there were any problems along the way.

"I always wanted to come here," Nick said. "We're close to the beaches where the Brits and Canadians landed on D-Day. They thought they'd take Caen on the first day but the Germans had other ideas. It took two months before the battle was over."

"Wasn't the city almost destroyed?" Selena asked.

"Yep. Like most of the towns and cities in Normandy. You really have to hand it to the men who fought here. House to house fighting, with German machine guns around every corner."

"Like Fallujah," Ronnie said.

Nick nodded. "Like that, except in Iraq they had AKs instead of MG-42s."

Germany had issued massive numbers of MG-42 machine guns to its troops in World War II. Wehrmacht small unit tactics had been built around the deadly guns. By contrast, few soldiers in the Allied armies carried automatic weapons back then, a logistical decision that cost many lives. Seventy some years later, Fallujah rolled around and everyone and his brother had automatic weapons. Nick and Ronnie had seen heavy fighting there. It had been hell on earth.

They passed a World War II cemetery where hundreds of white markers marched in neat rows across a manicured green lawn. The setting sun threw a soft, rose glow over the silent stones.

"Peaceful," Nick said as they drove past.

"Arlington's the same way," Lamont said.

"I think it's sad," Selena said.

"War is sad," Nick said.

No one said anything else for the next forty minutes.

Nick looked at his GPS. "We're getting close. Take the next left."

Selena turned onto a narrow country lane. Thick hedges lined the road on either side. Infrequent breaks in the shrubbery revealed fields lined with more hedges and an occasional farmhouse.

"Coming up on the right," Nick said. "Slow down a little."

The hedge gave way to a high stone wall that ran along the road for a hundred yards. A double gate of black iron stood closed at the entrance to the drive. The wall was high. The only view they got of the house was through the gate as they went by. There was time to see that the house was solid and large, two stories of stone with a gray slate roof. Then they were past.

"Cars parked in front of the house," Lamont said.

"Somebody's home," Ronnie said.

They passed the end of the wall. A tight row of tall hedges formed a right angle with the wall, going back toward the rear of the property. They crossed a short bridge over an irrigation canal filled with muddy water. The canal paralleled the hedges.

"Looks like the meeting is on. I'd better check in with Harker."

Nick activated his comm link.

"About time, Nick. What's your status?"

Harker's voice sounded tinny over the satellite relay.

"We've just passed the objective and are about to pull off the road."

He pointed at a dirt track that went from the road into a freshly plowed field. Selena drove onto the track and followed it to a copse of trees a hundred feet from the road. She pulled in under the trees and shut down the engine. From the road, it would be difficult to see them. They couldn't be seen at all from the villa.

"We're in a farmer's field near the objective," Nick said to Elizabeth. "Any updates for me?"

"Negative. Gutenberg got an email from Thorvaldson saying he'd be late, after eight."

"We won't be going in before then. So they'll all be there?"

"It looks that way," Elizabeth said.

"You sound like you're not sure."

"I don't know, Nick. This seems too pat, all of them in one place. Something doesn't feel right."

"Is that your intuition talking, Director?"

"These people are paranoid about security. Why are they meeting at that farmhouse, instead of Gutenberg's chalet or someplace secure?"

"Now you mention it, I had the same thought," Nick said. "But we have Gutenberg's emails. He couldn't know we're monitoring him."

"Just the same, be careful going in there."

"Have you got the infrared up?"

"Not yet. The satellite won't be in position for another hour and a half. Stephanie will relay it to you as soon as it comes online."

"Anything else?"

"No. Keep your head down," Elizabeth said.

"Copy that," Nick said.

CHAPTER 49

The team was all but invisible in their dark
gear. The only light came from a half moon that
shed a faint, silver glow on the freshly turned earth
of the fields. They crossed to the irrigation ditch
that ran along the side of Gutenberg's property. The
ditch was three feet wide. A short jump to the other
side brought them up against the hedges that
bordered the villa. Ronnie took a pair of heavy
brush clippers from his bag of tricks and began
working on the thick shrubbery.

"Stuff is like iron," he said under his breath.
His voice was an electronic whisper in their ears.
"Give me a couple of minutes."

It took five. Ronnie stepped back and Nick
peered through the opening. Several windows in the
villa showed light, all on the ground floor. The
upstairs was dark. Curtains drawn over the windows
made it impossible to see who or what was inside.
Nick toggled the comm link to Harker.

"Where's that infrared?" he said when she came
online.

"There's a big solar flare causing interference. I
can't get a clear signal. Satellite visual is out also."

Nick stuffed the urge to swear at her.

"All right. We're about to go in. Keep the line
open."

"Copy that. Good luck."

They'd all heard Elizabeth.

"How you want to do it?" Lamont said.

"The upstairs is dark. I'm thinking we could
climb up onto the gallery and get in from there. We

go in on the ground floor, they'll know we're there right away."

"Are we going to try and take them alive?" Selena asked.

"If we can," Nick said, "but it might not be possible. There have to be guards. Once they see us, they'll start shooting and all bets are off. We get into the house, toss flash bangs as soon as we see someone and clear the rooms. Shoot anyone who's armed. Don't hesitate. You hesitate, that's when someone will kill you."

"I know," she said. "You've told me often enough."

"Then I don't have to tell you again."

Selena started to say something and thought better of it.

"Seems odd there aren't any sentries," Lamont said. "You'd think they'd have some kind of perimeter lighting, at least."

"Yeah, you would," Nick said. "It bothers me too. It could be they don't want to draw any attention. Bright lights out here in the French countryside, someone would be sure to notice."

"Maybe," Lamont said.

"There could be ground sensors," Selena said.

"If there are sensors, there's nothing we can do about it," Nick said. "They'll send someone out of the house if we trigger an alarm. They might come out shooting."

Nick's ear began to itch. He tugged on it.

"I don't like this much," Ronnie said. "You're messing with your ear and we've got no Intel on what's inside that house."

Selena squatted next to Nick. "I don't like it either. Elizabeth is uneasy about this and so am I. Like Lamont said, why aren't there lights? Why aren't there sentries? These are powerful men, they wouldn't go anywhere without lots of security. Something's wrong."

"It smells like a setup to me," Lamont said. "It's too easy."

"Yeah," Ronnie said.

"All of you think it's a trap?"

They all nodded.

"All right. What's our next move?"

"Spring it, and see what happens," Ronnie said. "Maybe we'll learn something."

"How you gonna spring it without us getting killed?" Lamont asked.

Ronnie reached into his pack and pulled out the flash bangs.

"Three or four of these through the windows and see who comes out."

"The windows have curtains," Selena said, "How are you going to get those grenades through them?"

"We'll head for that far corner," Nick said. "None of the windows are lit back there. There has to be a back entrance. We'll go in through there. They can't surprise us if we know they're waiting."

"Room to room," Ronnie said.

"I hate houses," Lamont said.

"We don't have to go in," Ronnie said. "We open the door, we toss in grenades and wait. That ought to stir things up. We can follow up with something more serious than a flash bang if we have to."

"Sounds like a plan," Nick said. "Short and simple, I like it. Remember, there aren't any good guys inside that villa. Everyone in there is a legitimate target. Anyone have something to add?"

No one did.

He reached up to scratch his ear. "Okay, let's do it. Weapons free."

Kalicklickclick.

Four safeties came off as one.

They slipped through the opening in the hedge and sprinted for the back of the villa. They reached the end of the house with no sign of alarm. The tractor they'd seen in the satellite photo was parked behind the villa, between the house and the building with the wine press. There was a window high up on the wall of the building and a door directly opposite the villa. The door was partly open. Dim light showed through the opening.

"Better check that out first," Ronnie said.

They moved to the open door. Ronnie took a quick look.

"I don't see anyone. Take my six."

He stepped inside the building, Nick behind him.

The interior was a large, open space. A single bulb hung from the ceiling. There was a small office to the right and several tables. Massive hand-hewn beams of dark wood supported the roof. They looked as though they'd been there a long time. A large wooden tank stood near a set of high double doors at the far end that opened onto the vineyard beyond. Rows of wine barrels stacked two high and six across ran along both sides of the room. A main aisle went down the middle, with narrow aisles branching off between the barrels. There was no one there.

They went back outside. A heavy wooden door marked the rear entrance. Ronnie went to it and tried the handle. It clicked open. He raised his eyebrows and looked at Nick.

"Open it up and toss in a grenade," Nick said. His voice was quiet over the radio link.

Ronnie pulled open the door with a quick movement, ducked behind it and threw in a flash bang. He followed it up with another.

They looked away and covered their ears. The grenades went off with a deafening blast. The ground vibrated under their feet. Inside the house, someone screamed. Someone began firing. A stream of tracers poured through the open door.

"Up there," Selena yelled.

A man leaned out of a window and began firing at them with an automatic rifle, sending spurts of dirt from the ground at Selena's feet. She shot him. The rifle flew from his hand and he fell back out of sight.

A dark object came out of the house and landed between Lamont and Selena.

Lamont reached down, grabbed the grenade and hurled it away. He threw himself against Selena and took them both to the ground. Nick and Ronnie hit the dirt. The grenade detonated and sent a rain of dirt and rock over them.

Ronnie pulled a fragmentation grenade from his belt and threw it into the hallway beyond the open door. The explosion ripped through the night. More screams came from the house. Smoke billowed out of the opening.

The gunfire from the villa became constant, a steady ripping sound that sent hundreds of rounds toward them. Men began firing from windows on the second floor.

The house was a death trap. They kept firing and retreated behind the tractor. Bullets hammered into the metal with sharp, ringing sounds. It was poor shelter. They were too exposed.

"Into the winery," Nick yelled. "Lay down covering fire."

It was a short distance away. They ran for the open door, firing as they went. Lamont yelled and went down, his leg shot out from under him.

Selena let go with a long burst at the house as Nick and Ronnie grabbed Lamont and dragged him past her into the building. The bolt on her MP-5 locked open as she backed into the winery. Nick slammed the door shut behind her. Bullets thudded into the thick wood. Selena dropped the empty magazine and reloaded.

Ronnie was bent over Lamont, tying a makeshift bandage around a ragged wound on his lower leg.

"How bad?" he asked.

Lamont spoke between gritted teeth. Beads of sweat covered his forehead "I think the bone's broken. Hurts like a bastard."

"You want morphine?"

"Nah. Maybe later. After we get out of this."

"Now what?" Selena said.

Nick looked around.

"They'll be through that door pretty quick. They have to come in after us. Lamont, can you handle your rifle?"

"No problem. I just can't stand."

"Ronnie, you help Lamont and set him up to cover the door. Get behind those barrels over there. You take the other side. How's your ammo?"

"Still got plenty."

"I'm good," Lamont said.

"Selena, you take the same side as Lamont. I'm going to make sure they can't get through those doors in the back."

He turned and ran to the rear of the building. The big doors were closed but there was nothing to keep them from being pulled open. There were heavy U-shaped brackets on the doors. A long, heavy plank stood upright nearby. Nick lifted the plank and dropped it into the brackets. The doors were safe for the moment.

He moved to where Selena crouched behind one of the wine barrels. Something heavy slammed into the door they'd come through. It splintered and flew open.

Two men came through the broken door, rolled to the sides and came up firing. Covering fire came from outside. Bullets smashed into the rows of wine barrels, punching through the oak. Red streams of wine fountained out onto the floor.

Lamont leaned on a barrel, firing around it. Ronnie was on the other side. Everyone was shooting at once. The building filled with the sound of the guns.

Selena was caught up in the adrenaline high of the firefight. Almost as if something had taken control of her body, she moved out and shot one of the men who'd burst into the building. She felt like she'd stepped into a different dimension of time. Everything seemed to move in slow motion, except for her. She watched the second man start to turn his weapon toward her, his movements like a stylized ballet. She fired, felt the steady recoil in her wrists and arms. She watched the bullets stitch across his chest and drive him to the ground.

She ran toward the doorway. She felt powerful, invincible. She dropped a magazine and inserted another on the run.

"Shit!" Nick yelled. "Ronnie, go!"

Selena ran past the tractor, weaving and bobbing as fire from the house tried to bring her down. She ran through the open door toward a light at the end of a hallway. Someone came out of a room on the side, silhouetted against the light. She cut him down.

She reached the front room. Several men stared at her in surprise. Someone raised his weapon and fired. The rounds went past her with an eerie, whining sound. Her bullets took him in the chest and blew him backwards. She swung her MP-5 in a slow arc around the room, firing until the bolt locked back. She ejected the empty magazine and reached for another.

A man stood in the far corner aiming his rifle at her. Time speeded up again. Selena froze.

This is it, she thought. She fumbled with the magazine and waited for the impact.

Shots sounded behind her and the man spun and collapsed. Ronnie came up beside her.

"You all right?"

"I'm fine," she said. "Thanks."

"You're welcome."

Nick came up to her. He looked angry. "That was a damn stupid thing to do. What the hell is the matter with you?"

"Nick," Ronnie said. He put his hand on Nick's arm.

"It's all right, Ronnie," Selena said. "If he wants to be an asshole that's his problem."

"I count four dead bandits in here," Ronnie said. "Plus the ones we came through."

He walked over to one of the bodies.

"These guys look like mercenaries," he said. "The targets were never here. It was a setup."

"Gutenberg found out we were listening," Nick said.

"We made a lot of noise," Ronnie said. "We should get out of here."

"Then we'd better make it quick," Nick said. "Go get the van and bring it here. Selena and I will get Lamont."

"Copy that," Ronnie said. He went out the front door of the villa.

Nick said to Selena, "Why did you go in there like that?"

"It needed to be done."

"You got carried away, didn't you?"

She thought back on the feeling that had driven her out into the open. She'd felt fearless, as though she were an unstoppable force.

"I knew I wouldn't get hit," she said. "I wasn't thinking about it, it was a feeling and I went with it."

"You were in the zone."

"Yes."

"You almost got killed."

"Nothing new about that. I guess I'm finally getting used to it."

"I've been where you are," Nick said. "It's not good when you start thinking nothing can touch you. That's when you take risks. That's when you get hurt or killed."

"But I didn't, did I? Get hurt or killed."

"Not this time. Try to hear what I'm saying. You showed a lot of courage back there and I respect that. Hell, if we were in the service you'd get a medal. But most of the heroes I know are dead. I don't want you to be one of them."

Selena heard something in his voice that made her listen. At first she'd been angry because he'd seemed to criticize her. In hindsight, she saw it wasn't like that.

He's angry because he cares for me. He was afraid for me. That's different. Besides, maybe he's right.

She really didn't know why she'd jumped up and gone after those people like that. She hadn't thought about it. She'd just done it.

"It wasn't something I planned," she said.

Nick sighed. "I know, and that's what scares me. Acting without thinking can save your life but you have to watch out for believing you're invincible."

"I hear you. I'll think about it."

"That's good enough for me. Let's go find Lamont."

Lamont had gotten himself to the door. He was propped against a table, holding his rifle like a crutch and standing on his good leg. Blood stained the bandage Ronnie had wrapped around the wound.

"Figured it was cool when the shooting stopped," Lamont said.

His voice was strained. His coffee colored skin was pale.

"Take his good side," Nick said.

Selena took Lamont's MP-5 and slung it, then draped his right arm around her shoulders. Nick took Lamont's left. They moved out of the wine building toward the front of the villa. Selena heard the van coming up the gravel drive. In a moment Ronnie drove into the front yard.

Ronnie and Nick helped Lamont into the back of the van and laid him down.

"Ahh, watch the leg."

"We have to get out of our gear and back into civvies," Nick said. "Ronnie, let's get Lamont fixed up. We can't be seen like this."

In a few minutes they were changed into street clothes.

"Lamont, you want that morphine now?" Ronnie asked.

"Yeah. Send me to cloud land."

Ronnie took a morphine syrette from the first aid pack.

"Selena, you drive," Nick said.

"Where are we going?"

"Back to the plane."

"What about Lamont? He needs a hospital."

"We can't go to a hospital. How are we going to explain that wound? We have to get him back home. The bleeding is under control. We've got plasma on the plane and antibiotics. We'll splint his leg for now. Once we're in the air, it's only five or six hours. He'll be okay for that long. I'll call Harker and tell her to have an ambulance waiting."

"He's right, Selena," Lamont said. His voice was weak. "I'll be fine. Get us out of here."

An hour later they reached the airport. Nick had called ahead for the pilot to get the plane ready. A bored customs official took a casual look at their diplomatic papers and waved them through the gate to the private terminal where the Gulfstream waited.

Ten minutes later, they were in the air.

CHAPTER 50

Elizabeth looked up as Stephanie came into the room.

"Steph, what's the matter? You look like you just found a worm at the bottom of your coffee cup."

"I did find a worm, but it wasn't in my coffee. I got into the old KGB files, looking for more information about Vysotsky."

"And?"

"And, I discovered what he was doing back in the 80s."

"Something tells me I'm not going to like what you found," Elizabeth said.

"He was an assassin. Moscow used him for wet work abroad. He was one of the few agents trusted to work in the West."

"In America?"

"Yes. He was here in nineteen eighty-seven."

The date clicked in Elizabeth's head.

"You don't mean..."

"I do. Vysotsky is the one who killed Selena's family. He planted a device that released acid onto the brake lines on her father's car. The acid ate through the line, the brake fluid drained out and the next time her father hit the brakes it was all over. The car went through a guard rail and fell more than four hundred feet."

"How did he know when and where they were going?"

"Someone told him. The report refers to him as *Kolokol*. It means "bell" in Russian."

"That was the KGB code name for Aldrich Ames," Elizabeth said. "He set her father up to be killed."

Elizabeth opened a drawer at her desk and took out her aspirin bottle. She shook three into her hand and swallowed them with coffee.

"They should have shot him," Stephanie said.

"Ames? Yes, they should have. But we don't do that here. At least he'll never be a free man again."

"I don't think Selena will be satisfied with that."

"I'm not sure we should tell her," Elizabeth said. "It's bad enough that she found out her father had an affair with a Russian agent."

"Not to mention that she has a half-sister who's a Russian assassin."

"What a mess," Elizabeth said. "I'm not inclined to pile anything else on her."

"What about Vysotsky?"

"I wish I'd known this before. How come it didn't turn up in the past?"

"I found this on the SVR computers in Moscow. It was misfiled. Sometimes I wonder how the Russians ever get anything done, considering the size of their bureaucracy and the mistakes they make."

"That's excellent work, Steph."

"What about Vysotsky? It changes our relationship with him."

"It does," Elizabeth said, "but I can't say it surprises me. No one gets to his position of power in SVR without getting his hands dirty."

"Sometimes I wonder about our hands," Stephanie said. "Look at what we do. I tell myself we hold the boundaries, that there are things we won't do and that makes it all right. It helps me sleep at night."

"We make mistakes, Steph. It bothers me but the boundaries aren't set in stone. It's not a game. People who think civilized rules should always apply haven't a clue what it's like out there, where Nick and the others are. There aren't any neat moral and ethical lines."

"Sometimes I think there are only two kinds of people," Stephanie said. "The sheep and the shepherds. I guess we're shepherds."

"There are three kinds," Elizabeth said.

"What's the third?"

"The wolves. You forgot the wolves."

"It's hard to think of them as people."

"Speaking of wolves, Nick found a lair in France and took it out."

"What happened?"

"It was a trap. Nick said there were a dozen men waiting for them, hiding inside the house. Lamont was hit."

"How bad?" Stephanie asked.

"Bad enough. His leg's broken, he lost some blood. He's out of action."

"There's no way Gutenberg could have known we were coming."

"Then why were his men waiting for us?"

Stephanie looked thoughtful. "They might not have been waiting for us, exactly. He must have discovered the trace on his laptop. He'd want to know who was watching. Sending that email about the meeting in France was bait. It makes sense that whoever read it might go after him, and that's just what we did. All Gutenberg had to do was have his men in place and wait and see who showed up."

"The Russians didn't show up," Elizabeth said.

"That's curious, isn't it?"

"It makes me wonder how the Russian trace got on his computer in the first place. How easy would it be to tap in when he's online?"

"Not easy at all," Stephanie said. "Gutenberg isn't using some standard firewall to keep out hackers. He has one of the most sophisticated security protocols I've ever seen. It would take someone with my level of skill to get into it. I only discovered that trace by accident. It's possible someone else got past his encryption but I think it was planted directly onto his computer."

"Who would be able to do that? A man like Gutenberg isn't going to leave his computer lying around where anyone can get to it."

"He's been spending a lot of time in Paris," Stephanie said. "He stays at the George V every time he goes there. Maybe someone we don't know about is staying there with him."

"Does the hotel have CCTV cameras?"

"They must," Stephanie said. "Everyone does these days. I could get into them through the hotel computer. "

"Take a look and see if anyone looks interesting," Elizabeth said.

"It could be anyone he's with."

"My guess is that the person we're looking for will show up more than once."

Stephanie glanced at the clock. "It's getting late and I have a dinner engagement with Lucas. I'd like to tackle it tomorrow if that's okay with you."

"Tomorrow is soon enough," Elizabeth said.

CHAPTER 51

Gutenberg was on the phone with Jaques de Guillame, the French Foreign Minister, one of his allies on the board of AEON. Krivi, Thorvaldson and Kamarov were the others. He hadn't heard from Kamarov in days and he seemed to have vanished. In Russia that meant only one thing.

Gutenberg could feel the reins of power shifting. First the laboratory had been destroyed in Zürich. Then Valentina had betrayed him. And now his carefully planned trap had turned into a disaster. The failures were giving Senator Mitchell the opportunity he sought to ease Gutenberg from the leadership position. Mitchell didn't understand what Gutenberg would do to prevent that.

"Who was it? I want to know who it was," Gutenberg said.

"There is no positive identification," de Guillame replied. "However, I believe it was the Americans. A group of four Americans with diplomatic passports landed at Caen on the afternoon of the day your house was attacked. They left quite early the next morning. The customs official on-duty said one of the men appeared injured. The others had to help him onto the plane. The van they rented shows mileage consistent with a trip from the airport to your vineyard."

"Which Americans?"

"Who knows?" Gutenberg could almost feel the Frenchman shrug over the phone. "CIA, perhaps."

"Too risky for them," Gutenberg said. "You're sure it wasn't someone else? The Russians, for example?"

"Definitely not the Russians," de Guillame said.

"That is what I needed to know. Perhaps the American president's covert unit."

"I know about them. But it seems unlikely Rice would risk the embarrassment of failure."

"He would simply deny knowledge."

"What are you going to do, Johannes?"

"We continue with the plan but with a change in priority. Washington is more of a threat to us than the Chinese. I want to target America first. There's always time for Beijing."

"Mitchell isn't going to like that. You know he wants to hit the Chinese first."

"By the time he realizes what's happened, it will be too late. The disease will be well established and out of control."

"I thought we'd left these internal struggles behind. You know how destructive they've been in the past."

"It doesn't have to be that way this time," Gutenberg said. "It's up to Mitchell. He shouldn't have tried to undermine my leadership."

"You have my support. Just keep that damn stuff away from France," de Guillame said.

"Don't worry, Jaques. I see no advantage in targeting Europe. Some places have to be preserved. Besides, we live here. Krivi has already produced a large stockpile of vaccine. If by some mischance the disease reaches the continent, you will be well prepared and in position to use the situation to your advantage."

De Guillame chuckled. "You really should have been a politician, Johannes. You would have done quite well."

"I prefer the shadows," Gutenberg said. "I'll leave it to you to claim the spotlight."

"Please keep me informed," de Guillame said.

"Of course."

"Goodbye, Johannes."

In France, de Guillame set his phone down and thought about the conversation he'd just had. Johannes had sounded strained over the phone. Things had not gone well in the past weeks. Perhaps it was time to consider shifting his allegiance. A confrontation between Johannes and Mitchell was coming soon, he was sure of it. In the past, these struggles for power within the organization had caused many deaths and great disruption. It was important that he picked the right side.

He looked out the windows of his study at the verdant gardens and lawns surrounding his château. It was coming on dark, the light rapidly fading. Soft lights showed in the careful landscaping.

De Guillame's mansion was in the Paris suburb of Versailles. He'd inherited the estate from his father, but if that had not been the case he would have chosen to live here anyway. Versailles had always been a seat of power in France. It was fitting that he lived there.

The Versailles Palace was not far away and De Guillame was fond of visiting the magnificent building. He looked out the study windows at his garden and let himself imagine what it must have been like to be king, before the revolution. He would have enjoyed being king.

Absorbed in his fantasy, de Guillame failed to notice a dark figure slip into the study. It wasn't until the thin wire of a garrotte slipped over his head and bit into his throat that he realized anyone else was there.

He choked and gasped and scrabbled with his fingers at the wire, trying to reach the hands that were killing him. Blood ran down under the collar of his tailored blue shirt.

"Dos'vedanya," a soft voice whispered in his ear.

Valentina waited until de Guillame's feet stopped kicking. She unwrapped the wire from his neck, wiped it clean on his jacket sleeve and replaced the garrotte in a pouch at her belt. She went to the doors leading into the garden and slipped away into the dark.

CHAPTER 52

Selena and Nick stood in the empty loft that was soon to be their home. They'd signed the contract and were waiting for the escrow to close. The agent had been ecstatic at the sale. She'd given them a key, even though ownership wasn't yet official.

The view across the Potomac to Virginia was better today than it had been the first time they'd seen it. Everything had turned green across the river. Nick walked over and opened a window. A fresh, spring breeze brought the scent of blossoms into the space. Selena joined him. He put his arm around her.

"This is great," he said. "I didn't realize how much I missed looking at something besides apartment buildings."

"I really like the river view. It's wonderful."

"I've got someone lined up to take over my lease as soon as I'm out of there," he said.

She turned and looked at the open space and saw a blank slate begging to be filled. The brick walls were clean, the wood floors glowing with rich, warm color. The room was filled with sunlight streaming through the windows facing the river. Four peaked skylights let more light in through the ceiling.

"That wall is perfect to hang the paintings I had shipped from San Francisco," she said. "I'd like to get the security installed before anything else. Then we can decide about movers and furniture and all that."

"I was thinking the same thing about the security."

"I wish it wasn't necessary," Selena said.

"It's the nature of things. It's always been that way."

"Did you talk with Elizabeth this morning?"

"Yes. Lamont's pretty messed up," Nick said. "The round shattered one of the bones. They put the pieces back together but it's uncertain how it's going to turn out."

"Will he be able to walk?"

"Oh yeah, that's not the problem. The question is how well."

"Let's go see him later."

"I thought we'd go this morning. Harker wants us to come in this afternoon. Someone assassinated the French Foreign Minister last night. He was one of the men named in Gutenberg's diary."

"Who killed him?"

"Nobody knows. It was a professional hit. Someone got into his house and took him out."

"I suppose I should be shocked," she said, "but I'm not. I'm just glad we didn't have to go after him."

"Things aren't going too well for AEON right now. It makes me nervous."

"Why?"

"AEON is like a wounded animal and that makes it unpredictable. What's Gutenberg going to do? What's happening with the rest of the leadership? How does de Guillame's death change things?"

"We've never known what they're going to do."

"Yes, but there was a kind of predictability in their thinking. Now we don't even have that."

"We know one thing," Selena said. "There's another player in the game. The Russians. Maybe they assassinated de Guillame. They're good at assassinating people."

There was a hard note in Selena's voice. Nick chose to overlook it. He looked at his watch.

"We ought to get going if we want to see Lamont before we meet with Harker."

As he locked the door behind him he wondered what would happen if Selena ever met her half sister. He hoped he never had to find out.

CHAPTER 53

Elizabeth had decided not to tell Selena that General Vysotsky was the man who had killed her father. She and Stephanie were the only two people who knew. And Vysotsky, but it was certain he wouldn't be talking to Selena about it.

Ronnie, Nick and Selena sat across from Elizabeth on the couch. Stephanie sat to the side of Elizabeth's desk with her laptop open.

"Another one of AEON's directors is dead. Aapo Thorvaldson's body was found this morning."

"How did he die?" Nick asked.

"It looks like a heart attack but I think he was murdered. First de Guillame, now Thorvaldson. Two of AEON's leaders dying within a day of each other is too much of a coincidence."

"Somebody is saving us a lot of trouble," Ronnie said.

"It has to be the Russians," Nick said. "They're getting even."

"That's my guess," Elizabeth said.

"Who's left?" Selena asked.

"Gutenberg of course, and Krivi Dass. As far as we know both of them are still fine. The other names we have are Halifax, Mitchell and Kamarov. Kamarov has disappeared. The Russians probably picked him up."

"Then there are only four left," Nick said.

"It's going to be harder to go after them now that they know someone is targeting them," Elizabeth said

"They knew that after we hit the Zürich lab."

"That wasn't the same as going after them on a personal level," Elizabeth said.

"Why not wait and let the Russians or whoever kill the rest of them?" Ronnie said.

"We can't count on that." Elizabeth brushed a speck of lint from her sleeve. "Another problem is that we don't know for sure that Halifax and Mitchell are who we think they are. We can't go after the British Chancellor of the Exchequer or an American senator based on a suspicion."

"What about Krivi?" Nick said. "We know he's one of them. Or Gutenberg."

"Of the two, Krivi is a better choice."

"Why not Gutenberg?"

"Krivi knows everything about the disease. If we grab him we might find out how to stop it."

"I haven't seen much about it on the news," Ronnie said.

"You won't. The media have been told to stay away from it."

"Unofficial reports say twelve thousand people have died in Brazil and that the disease is out of control," Stephanie said.

"I've seen a couple of television interviews with those slick doctors the government trots out every time people wonder if there's going to be an epidemic," Nick said. "They always say the same thing. It's not coming here, we're prepared if it does, and you have nothing to worry about anyway. All those confident statements make me nervous."

"Is it coming here?" Selena asked.

"Yes, if Gutenberg has his way," Elizabeth said. "America and China are the prime targets."

Selena said, "It's crazy. What do they hope to gain? Money? What's their goal?"

"Money is only part of it. They want to reduce the world population to something they can control more easily. AEON thinks there are too many people in the world, especially from what they call inferior races."

"They don't consider Krivi to be part of an inferior race?" Ronnie asked. "He's got brown skin."

"By definition, he has to be superior or he wouldn't be part of AEON's leadership," Elizabeth said.

Ronnie snorted. "That's convenient. Kind of like Hitler making the Japanese honorary Aryans."

"You can't expect them to be rational," Elizabeth said. "They're sociopaths."

"Let's get back to the mission," Nick said.

"There's a good reason for us to go after Krivi next," Elizabeth said. "He developed a vaccine or they wouldn't have let it loose. He knows how to make it. You have to try and take him alive."

"That might be easier said than done," Nick said. "Where is he now?"

"India," Stephanie said. "He lives in Mumbai. That's where his drug factories are and that's where the vaccine will be."

She typed in a command on her keyboard. Pictures of Krivi's home appeared on the monitor.

"This is his house," she said.

The building was long and low, stepping down to a second level on the side of a landscaped hill. The roof was covered in red tile. The walls were whitewashed, the grounds green and shaded. It looked inviting, expensive and peaceful. A colonnade of arches paraded across the front of the building. The view from the back of the house looked out over the polluted waters of the Back Bay.

"Krivi lives on Malabar Hill. It's one of the most expensive places to live in the world. An apartment there will run you eight or nine thousand dollars a square foot."

Ronnie let out a low whistle.

"Everyone who's powerful or famous or rich wants to live there," Stephanie said. "Bollywood film stars, the high government officials, the captains of industry. The super rich. Mumbai is the wealthiest city in India."

"And the poorest," Selena said. "There are over nine million people living in slums."

"I don't think Krivi cares about that," Stephanie said.

Nick pointed at the picture on the monitor. "It's going to be hard to approach the house across those lawns. He's got security cameras everywhere. That low building on the right looks like it could be guard quarters."

"I'll bet he's got laser sensors and motion detectors too," Ronnie said.

"We'll decide how to go after him once we're there," Nick said

"I think we are running out of time. Brazil was just a test," Elizabeth said. "Now that they know it works, they'll move on to the next part of their plan."

"Which is?" Nick asked.

"Release it here or in China."

"Then I guess we'd better go talk to Krivi," Nick said.

CHAPTER 54

Alexei Vysotsky's new position as deputy director of SVR put him under close scrutiny by the Kremlin. That was nothing unusual. He hadn't survived this long without understanding how the game was played. What the Kremlin wanted was results, and Alexei intended to give them what they wanted. So far, things had gone well. Along with Kamarov, two of AEON's leaders had been eliminated. The others would be more difficult. If for Vysotsky, difficulties were only obstacles to be overcome.

He took a pad of paper and wrote down the names of the remaining four men who ran AEON.

Mitchell
Halifax
Gutenberg
Dass

The logistics of these things could become complicated, but Vysotsky believed in keeping it simple. The best way was to get close to the target, one on one. It was an effective tactic and required only careful planning by the agent. A prick with the tip of a poisoned umbrella as the target walked by. A tasteless drug slipped into a cocktail. A quick, silenced bullet to the back of the head. A slim stiletto between the ribs. The garrotte. Alexei had personal experience with all of them.

He thought about Valentina. She'd done well in France, first by compromising Gutenberg's computer and then eliminating the French Foreign

Minister. He decided she would be the best choice to go after the American senator. Senator Mitchell had a reputation as a philanderer, though his adoring constituents knew nothing of his liaisons. It should be easy for Valentina to catch his eye. The rest would follow as night followed day.

He wrote her name next to Mitchell's.

With Mitchell disposed of in his thinking, Vysotsky turned his attention to Halifax, the British Chancellor of the Exchequer. After the Prime Minister, Halifax was the most important government official in England. He had strong security around him at all times. He would not be a simple target, but Vysotsky knew that a determined assassin could not be stopped.

Halifax was a public man and his death would create a storm of suspicion. The deaths of several prominent billionaires within days of one another meant there was a risk someone could make a connection between them. The deaths formed a pattern. Patterns meant vulnerability.

Alexei made a note to wait on Halifax.

That left Gutenberg and the Indian, Dass. The two men lived in virtual fortresses but both commuted, Gutenberg to his bank in Geneva and Dass to his factories in Mumbai. It would be possible for a team to get them as they traveled to work.

Mumbai was one of the most crowded cities in the world, filled with impossible traffic, confusion and countless opportunities for an ambush. Geneva was a city with excellent police, surveillance everywhere and little in the way of significant cover.

It wasn't a difficult choice. Vysotsky decided to delay going after Gutenberg.

Dass would be the next target. An operation out on the open road required a different kind of approach, using a team with a skilled driver and at least one shooter. There were several in Zaslon who were ruthless and efficient enough to organize and lead the operation.

Alexei picked up his phone.

CHAPTER 55

"There he is," Nick said.

He handed the binoculars to Ronnie. Krivi Dass had just come out of his house. He walked down a short flight of steps flanked by three bodyguards and got into the back seat of a white Rolls-Royce. The driver closed the door behind him, got into the front and pulled away.

"Nice ride," Ronnie said.

"He can afford it," Nick said.

They'd rented a silver Mercedes at the airport, something that wouldn't look out of place in the high-end neighborhood where Krivi lived. The air-conditioning struggled against the merciless heat outside. At 10 o'clock in the morning, it was already 107° and climbing. The humidity of Southern India clung to them inside the confines of the car.

They'd decided it was easier to go after Krivi away from his home. Nick was behind the wheel. Selena sat next to him in front. Ronnie was in the back. Nick waited until the Rolls was almost out of sight before pulling out after him.

"Must be hard to live here year round, with this heat," Ronnie said. "It's not even the hottest part of the year yet."

"Not so hard if you were born here," Selena said. "It's Europeans that have trouble."

They followed Krivi's car through residential streets leading away from Malabar Hill to an intersection with a road called the Sion Panvel highway. The Rolls headed west. Nick kept three or four cars behind.

They came to a six lane divided highway marked as the Eastern Express Highway. The white Rolls turned south and headed toward Mumbai.

"Looks like he's going to work," Selena said.

Nick was in the center lane. Traffic was heavy and moving fast. A dark blue Toyota van sped past them on the right. The windows were blacked out.

"He's in a hurry," Ronnie said.

"He's coming up on Krivi," Selena said.

The van cut to the left and pulled alongside Krivi's car. The cargo door on the side of the van slid open. Two men leaned out with automatic weapons and began firing at the Rolls.

"Shit," Ronnie said.

The windows along the side of the Rolls-Royce disintegrated in a shower of glass. Holes appeared in the expensive coach work, dark spots peppering the gleaming white paint. The bullets found the driver and Krivi's car swerved in a sudden impossible turn and rolled. Pieces of metal and glass fountained into the air. The heavy car rolled again toward a concrete divider in the middle of the highway and smashed to a stop.

The blue van accelerated away. Nick dodged the debris and passed the wreck. Krivi's car was totaled. Cars swerved right and left around them, trying to miss the jagged pieces of metal littering the roadway. Nick cut the wheel left, missing a braking taxi. In the rearview mirror, what was left of the Rolls-Royce burst into flame. Black, ugly smoke roiled into the sky.

Ahead, the blue van was still in sight. Nick floored it. The Mercedes leapt ahead.

"Lock and load," he said.

"You want to go after them? What about Krivi?" Selena asked.

"He's dead. We need to know who took him out."

"Probably the same people who killed the others," Ronnie said.

"Yeah, but who are they?"

"We're outgunned," Ronnie said.

"What's your point?"

"Just sayin'."

Ronnie took out his pistol and racked the slide.

Ahead, the tall buildings of Mumbai's city center were getting close. They came up behind the blue van. Nick was thinking about his next move when the rear doors opened. Someone knelt in the back, leveling a rifle at them.

Nick pulled right just as the man fired. The bullets blew out the windshield of a truck behind them. The truck plowed into the side of a bus, driving it off the road. Behind them traffic disintegrated into chaos.

Ronnie leaned out of his window and began firing at the van.

"Get the tires," Nick yelled.

He swerved again as bullets struck the side of the Mercedes. Ronnie fired and the shooter toppled onto the roadway. The Mercedes ran over him with a dull, double thump.

Selena opened the sunroof and stood up through it, her Sig held firm in both hands. She emptied the magazine at the open doors of the blue van and dropped back into the car. The van accelerated into the outside lane, out of control. It struck the low divider and flipped over it onto the opposite side of the highway, straight into the path of a oncoming tractor trailer. The huge truck plowed into the van and pushed it along the pavement in a shower of sparks and screeching metal.

They were going fast. On the other side of the highway, the scene receded in the rearview mirror.

"Now what?" Ronnie asked.

"Now we find a place to dump this car," Nick said. "Someone will have seen us shooting at the van. The police will be looking for it."

"It won't be hard to get rid of it," Ronnie said. "Leave it on the edge of the slums with the keys in it. It'll be gone in minutes."

"That's cynical, Ronnie," Selena said.

"That's reality. Mumbai is no different than Detroit or LA."

"We're getting close to the dock area where Krivi's factory is," Selena said.

"I hear sirens," Ronnie said.

"They don't sound like cops," Nick said.

"Something's on fire over there." Selena pointed at a thick column of smoke rising somewhere ahead.

Two fire engines screamed by, then another, headed toward the smoke. Nick followed the trucks, turned a corner and pulled to a stop. A long, three-story brick building burned with red-hot heat. Tongues of fire roared from the windows of the second and third floors. As they watched, flames burst through the roof. More sirens sounded in the distance. A sign was painted along the top of the building.

DASS PHARMACEUTICALS MUMBAI, INDIA

"This can't be a coincidence." Selena watched two firemen unrolling a hose.

"If Krivi was stockpiling vaccine it was probably in that building," Nick said.

"Won't be doing anybody much good now," Ronnie said.

"Let's go home," Nick said.

CHAPTER 56

Johannes Gutenberg listened to the report of Krivi's death and resisted the urge to hurl his phone across the room. Instead, he forced himself to place it gently on his desk.

Someone was killing the leadership of AEON. First Kamarov had disappeared. Then de Guillame had been strangled and Thorvaldson had a convenient heart attack. Now, Krivi. It was down to Mitchell, Halifax and himself and it didn't take a genius to see the pattern. He needed to create a problem bigger than himself for whoever was behind the attacks.

Gutenberg depressed a button on his intercom.

"Yes, sir." The voice of his personal assistant came through the speaker.

"Get hold of Schmidt. I want to see him now."

"Yes sir. I think he's in the billiards room."

"Just get him in here." Gutenberg turned off the intercom.

Some minutes later Schmidt came into the study, his face flushed from hurrying.

"I was outside," he said. "Your secretary said it was urgent."

"We have a problem," Gutenberg said. "Krivi's dead."

"How?"

"He was ambushed on the highway as he was going to his office. They also torched his factory. Our stockpiles of vaccine were inside."

"Do you have any idea who's behind these attacks?"

"No. It could be the Americans. Maybe the Russians. At the moment, I don't really care. It's time to initiate the next phase."

"China?"

"No. I want to release the plague on the East Coast of America. We'll start with local exposure. New York should get things rolling nicely."

"Is that wise? With Krivi gone, it will take time to build up our supplies of vaccine again. It could get over here before we're ready."

"How long will it take to replenish our stockpiles?"

"Two months. Perhaps three."

"Have all of our essential personnel been vaccinated?"

"Of course."

"Then I'm not going to worry about it."

"Have you told Mitchell what you plan?"

"He can find out like everybody else, by watching the news."

*****

At that moment, Senator Randolph Mitchell wasn't watching the news. He was watching a seductive young woman sitting down at the bar in one of his favorite restaurants. It was possible she was one of the high-end hookers who trolled the power spots of Washington but there was something about her that made him think otherwise. He signaled the waiter over.

"Senator."

"Have you noticed that young lady at the bar?"

"It would be hard not to, sir."

"Have you seen her before?"

"No, Senator."

"Please ask her if she would like to join me for a cocktail."

As the waiter crossed the room toward the bar, Mitchell contemplated what she was going to be like when he got her into bed. That she would be there before midnight, he had no doubt. The combination of power, immense wealth and good looks that Mitchell possessed made him nearly irresistible. He had long ago cultivated an easy charm that smoothed the way for his conquests. He was adept at telling women what they wanted to hear and handsome enough to make it easy to listen.

She looked over at him as the waiter indicated Mitchell's table. She had intense, blue eyes and full, red lips. Mitchell smiled at her.

Valentina came over to his table. Mitchell stood.

"Thank you for joining me," he said. "Please, sit down." He indicated the chair next to his.

"Are you really a senator?" she said as she sat. Her voice was deep, soft. She had a faint accent he couldn't quite place, something European.

Wonderful, he thought. *She really doesn't know who I am.*

"Guilty," he said. "Randolph Mitchell."

"Jacqueline DuMons," Valentina said.

Mitchell sat and signaled the waiter. "Where are you from, Jacqueline?"

"It is that obvious? That I am not from here?"

"Not at all, but I thought I heard a trace of an accent. Are you French, perhaps?"

"Now it is my turn to say guilty," she said. "Yes, I live in Paris. I have a flat in Montmarte."

The waiter arrived at the table.

"What are you having?" Mitchell said.

"Whatever you are."

"Two martinis, Joseph, very dry."

"Very good, Senator."

"This is a very nice restaurant," Valentina/Jacqueline said, looking around.

"The food is excellent. Would you care to join me for dinner? I think food is always better when it's shared, don't you? Like many things."

Valentina looked at him and smiled. "Are you making a proposition at me, Senator?"

Mitchell laughed. "In America, we would say making a pass, not a proposition. Why don't we see how the evening progresses?"

You didn't answer my question, you lecher, Valentina thought. *But then, I already know the answer.*

The waiter brought their drinks.

Mitchell raised his glass toward her. "To new acquaintances."

He drank. She sipped and set her glass down next to his.

A man in his 40s in an expensive suit approached the table.

"Senator, I need a word."

Mitchell turned to look at him.

Valentina wore a ring in the shape of a rose. When Mitchell turned she reached for her purse and passed her hand over his glass, touching the top of the ring. A clear drop of liquid fell from the ring into his drink. The poison was one of the products of SVR's laboratories. It caused total paralysis of the vocal cords and respiratory system. The victim could neither speak nor breathe. The poison would take effect almost instantly.

It was an extremely unpleasant way to die.

"Not now, Maury," Mitchell said to the man in the suit. "Call my secretary tomorrow and make an appointment. Tell her I said ten minutes."

"Senator..."

"Tomorrow, Maury." There was an edge in Mitchell's voice. He turned back toward Valentina. "I apologize for the interruption."

"No need to apologize," Valentina said. "A powerful man has many distractions."

Mitchell picked up his martini and drained half the glass.

"Shall we order?"

Mitchell started to raise his arm to signal the waiter. His face contorted in agony. He clutched his chest, eyes bulging. His mouth gaped open and closed as his body spasmed. Mitchell struggled to his feet and fell sideways, grabbing the tablecloth and pulling glasses and silverware down on top of him.

Valentina let out a scream and stood, backing away from the table with her hands to her mouth. In the rush to Mitchell's side, all eyes were on the stricken man. Valentina melted away into the crowd. By the time anyone thought to look for the beautiful young woman who had been having a drink with the senator, she was blocks away.

CHAPTER 57

Nick, Ronnie and Selena were in Lamont's hospital room. It was eight in the morning. The remains of a mediocre institutional breakfast curdled on a tray near his bedside.

"Nick, you guys gotta get me some decent food. This stuff can make you sick."

"If it does, you're in the right place," Ronnie said.

"Yeah, right."

"Next time we come, we'll bring you a pizza," Nick said.

"How's your leg, Shadow?" Selena asked.

"The doc said it's going to take a few months to heal. The bone was busted up pretty bad. He said I'll have a permanent limp. It could've been worse. They almost had to amputate."

No one said anything for a moment.

"I've been thinking," Lamont said.

"There you go again with that thinking stuff," Ronnie said. "You have to stop doing that. It only confuses you."

"No, seriously. I'm tired of spending time in places like this and I'm getting too damn old to take any more hits like this one. It's time for me to quit."

They all started talking at once.

"Lamont..."

"What do you mean..."

"We need you..."

"Hey," Lamont said. "My mind's made up. I'm getting too beat up to keep doing this. It's going to take months for the strength to come back in my leg and even when it does, I won't be able to move like

I used to. I'd be a liability. Besides, I'm tired of getting shot at."

"You sound certain," Nick said.

"I am."

Their pagers went off. Nick looked at the display. "Harker just sent a 911," he said to Lamont. "We have to go. We'll talk about this the next time we see you."

"Sure. Just remember to bring that pizza."

Lamont watched his friends go. A sudden wave of pain shot up his leg. He pressed the call button for the nurse.

Going down in the elevator, Nick said, "I knew this had to happen sooner or later. I just didn't know who would be first."

"Maybe he'll change his mind," Selena said.

"I don't think so," Nick said. "He has a point about the leg. If he can't cut it physically he'd put himself and us at risk. He might not worry much about himself but he'd never do something to jeopardize us."

"How are we going to replace him?" Ronnie asked.

"I don't know."

"I wonder what Harker wants?" Selena said.

"We'll find out soon enough."

When they got to headquarters, Elizabeth and Stephanie were waiting for them.

"About time," Elizabeth said.

"We were visiting Lamont," Nick said. "What's up, Director?"

"Senator Randolph Mitchell was assassinated last night."

"Who killed him?"

Elizabeth cast a sideways glance at Stephanie. "The Russians. It was Valentina Antipov. Videos from the security cameras at the restaurant caught her dropping something in his drink."

Oh, oh, Nick thought.

Selena's face closed down. "You're certain? There can't be a mistake?"

"No. There's no doubt at all."

"I can't believe this," she said.

"We're monitoring terminals out of the city but she's probably already gone."

Stephanie said, "We weren't sure Mitchell was part of AEON. Now we are."

Elizabeth said, "It was the Russians who hit Krivi as well. I spoke with the deputy director of India's intelligence agency earlier. The people who killed him were using AK's, which doesn't tell us anything. But they found Spetsnaz tattoos on two of the bodies."

"Do the Indians know we're the ones who took them out?"

"I didn't think they needed to know that. They're still upset about what happened when you were there before. There's more."

"I can't wait to hear it," Ronnie said.

Harker gave him one of her hard looks.

"Krivi's chief research scientist landed at Kennedy this morning. He's traveling with a false passport under the name of Kurtz."

"Schmidt?" Nick said. "The guy we followed in Zürich?"

"The same."

"What's he doing here?"

"That's the question isn't it?" Elizabeth fiddled with her pen. "I'm sending you to New York to find out."

"How do we find one man in the middle of New York City?"

"He checked into a midtown hotel, one of those boutique places that compete with the big names. You can start there."

"What do you want us to do when we find him?"

"Take him someplace where you won't be bothered and ask him a few questions. Find out why he's here. Be careful. Remember, he's the one who plays with plague. I'm sure he's protected against it, but you aren't. Find out if there are any supplies of vaccine that weren't in Krivi's factory."

"What's happening in Brazil?" Selena asked.

"The plague is spreading. The Brazilian government quarantined the infected area but some carriers slipped through the roadblocks. The first cases have appeared in two cities along the northern coast. If we don't find a way to stop it soon, it's going to kill a lot of people."

"Is there any progress on a cure?"

"CDC is working around the clock. So is the World Health Organization. The best medical researchers in the world are trying to find a way to stop it. The White House is putting pressure on the North Koreans for information but no one's holding their breath waiting for an answer. Pyongyang's official line is that they don't know anything about it and anyone who says differently is part of a vicious attack by the warmongering, capitalistic West."

"Yeah, right," Ronnie said.

"Hood sent a team to Zürich. They're raiding Krivi's corporate headquarters tonight. There's bound to be something there about the vaccine. They'll find it and bring it back."

"If the Russians hadn't decided to interfere, that bug would still be locked up somewhere in the mountains of North Korea," Selena said.

"Vysotsky has a lot to answer for," Elizabeth said. "In the meantime, go find Schmidt."

CHAPTER 58

The clerk at the hotel desk seemed mesmerized by Selena's breasts.

"Mister Kurtz? Yes, he checked in yesterday. But he's not here at the moment."

"Oh?" Selena resisted the urge to slap him. "Do you know when he'll be back?"

"He's gone to the Metropolitan Museum. The hotel provides tickets for guests as part of our current promotion. Would you like to leave a message?"

"No. No message."

Nick and Ronnie waited for her outside the lobby entrance.

"The desk clerk is a creep," Selena said. "Kurtz isn't there. He's gone to the Met."

"The museum?" Nick asked.

"Is there another Met in New York?"

"The opera."

"Mets. Baseball team," Ronnie said.

Selena ignored him. "I don't think Kurtz is here to go sightseeing."

Nick stepped into the street and waved for a cab. Three ignored them before one stopped. They climbed in. The driver wore a full, bushy beard and a wool watch cap in rainbow colors. The car smelled of spicy takeout food and sweat. Nick rolled down his window.

"The Met."

The driver grunted, started the meter and turned out into traffic. They were on Lexington Avenue at forty-ninth. The museum was blocks away at seventy-fifth, across from Central Park on Fifth Avenue.

Shocks in the taxi were a thing of the distant past. The car crawled through the Manhattan traffic, jolting Nick's spine with every pothole.

"What's the plan?" Ronnie asked.

"Find Schmidt and get him somewhere private."

"The museum is a big place and it's going to be crowded," Selena said. "He could be anywhere."

"That's what worries me," Nick said. "The Koreans were working on an aerosol delivery system for the plague. What if Schmidt is here to release it? All he has to do is find a crowded room and spray it into the air. Everyone would be infected. In a few weeks half the city would be down with it."

"That's a terrible thought," Selena said.

The taxi let them off at the foot of the broad steps leading up to the museum. Huge banners hung on the front of the building, announcing a special exhibition in Impressionist art. They climbed the steps and Nick handed over seventy-five dollars for three tickets. Inside, the cavernous entrance hall echoed with footsteps and voices. An octagonal marble information desk with literature and maps sat front and center. The many wings and galleries of the museum lay beyond.

Nick got maps from the desk and a handout on the Impressionist exhibition. He kept one of the maps and handed the others to Selena and Ronnie.

Ronnie looked at his map. "There are hundreds of rooms in here. How do we find him?"

"We can't look in every room," Selena said. "It would take all day."

"You have any ideas where to start?" Nick said.

"Where are the most people going to be?"

"Probably at that special exhibition."

"Then let's start there."

Nick consulted the handout. "It's on the second floor."

They took the stairs to the second floor. Signs pointed to the left for the exhibition. They passed through a room displaying drawings and prints from the thirteenth and fourteenth centuries. The next gallery was hung with photographs. They turned right through another gallery of photographs and entered the special exhibition hall.

"How are we going to take him, if he's in here?" Selena asked. "The room's full of people."

"Carefully," Nick said. "Very carefully."

They scanned the room.

"I don't see him," Selena said.

"Let's check out the far side."

They worked their way through the crowd.

"I think that's him," Ronnie said. "In front of that painting over there."

Schmidt stood in front of a large canvas by Vincent van Gogh. His hands were out of sight, clasped in front of him. The painting was alive with inner light. There wasn't much on the canvas. A few dark lines suggested a plowed field. Dark birds circled in the sky. A vibrant sun blazed down with white heat from an endless sky.

Nick came up to Schmidt and stood next to him, looking at the canvas. Ronnie and Selena were a few steps away on either side.

"Beautiful, isn't it?" Schmidt said. "This is one of van Gogh's last paintings. He was mad by then, almost at the end. The crows in the sky tell you that. I know who you are, Carter. I saw you and the others come in."

Nick suppressed his surprise. "Then you know why I'm here."

"You're here for this."

Schmidt held up a silver aerosol canister he'd been concealing in his hands. His thumb covered a red button on the side of the can.

"You can't stop me, you know. The contents of this can are under extremely high pressure. If I press the button or drop the can it will discharge. You know what happens when someone coughs or sneezes? Microscopic droplets explode from the nostrils and mouth at over two hundred miles an hour. This is more powerful than that. Everyone in this room will be exposed."

"So will you," Nick said.

How do I get it away from him?

"But I'm protected. You aren't."

He held the can up.

"Mister, are you going to make graffiti on that picture?"

The disapproving voice came from a young girl, about ten years old.

For just an instant, Schmidt was distracted. It was long enough. Nick delivered a hard upward chop to Schmidt's wrist. The lethal can flew high into the air, tumbling in a lazy arc as it started down toward the floor. Ronnie dove headlong and caught it just as it was about to land.

Schmidt cursed and drove his elbow into Nick's gut, doubling him over. The girl screamed.

Selena moved in. Schmidt launched a kick toward her hip. He caught her off balance and knocked her down. Around them, people backed away. Schmidt ran for the door and Selena bounded to her feet and ran after him. She caught him at the entrance with a sweeping kick that took his legs out from under him. Schmidt rolled, pulled out a pistol and fired at her. She swept the gun from his hand with her leg and kicked the side of his head with the steel toe of her shoe. Something cracked, the sound loud and ugly. Schmidt's eyes rolled back. Blood trickled from his mouth.

People were screaming and running out of the hall.

Nick ran up to her. "You all right?"

"He missed. I'm all right, but he isn't."

On the floor, Schmidt's body convulsed. His feet beat a short tattoo on the floor. He let out a gurgling sound and died.

"I wish you hadn't killed him," Nick said.

"I didn't mean to. I went on automatic."

"Don't worry about it."

Ronnie came over, holding the canister as if it were a bomb about to explode.

"Nice catch," Nick said.

"I used to play center field."

"You haven't lost the touch."

"He was really going to let that stuff go, wasn't he?" Selena said.

"He was. If that little girl hadn't come up, I don't think I could've stopped him."

The vast exhibition hall was almost empty, except for museum guards watching them and keeping their distance. The guards weren't armed. It would be only minutes before the police arrived.

"We better get out of here while we can," Ronnie said, "unless you want to answer a lot of questions."

"Too late," Selena said. "The cops are here."

"FREEZE!" The shout echoed in the empty hall. Half a dozen police had their guns out and pointed in their direction.

"Harker is going to hate this," Ronnie said.

CHAPTER 59

"Can't you ever do something without making a public spectacle out of yourselves?"

Elizabeth looked cool and efficient in her tailored black pants suit and white blouse. Her cat-like green eyes flashed with annoyance.

"We didn't have much of a choice, Director," Nick said. He rubbed his chin, feeling a two-day stubble. There hadn't been time to shave.

They were back in Virginia. It had taken serious pressure and the invocation of the magic words *National Security* before the NYPD would let them go.

"I sent the canister down to CDC in Atlanta. Now that they have a sample it will be easier to find a way to defeat it. That's the good news. The bad news is that Gutenberg is still out there. He's not going to quit just because Schmidt didn't succeed."

"I can guess what you're going to say next," Nick said.

"He must have more of the plague stashed somewhere and we need to find it. You're going to Switzerland. Gutenberg is holed up in his château. "

"Here are the satellite shots," Stephanie said. The wall monitor lit.

"Fancy digs," Ronnie said.

The château was four stories high, set on a bump of land sticking out like a thumb into the Rhône. Tall, pointed towers and spires gave it a fairytale quality. It looked as if it belonged in a movie about arrogant nobles and men with plumed hats and long swords.

A tree-lined drive led to a high, stone wall and an iron gate that opened into a large, paved courtyard. There was a guardhouse outside the gate and a large fountain in the middle of the courtyard. The wall was topped with jagged pieces of glass and ran all the way around the building. In the back, the wall descended past ground level to the river's edge. A heavy retaining wall foundation kept the château from crumbling into the river.

"It was built early in the eighteenth century," Stephanie said. "There are over a hundred and fifty rooms."

"Perfect for that casual weekend get-together," Ronnie said.

"Here are the original plans," Stephanie said. She touched her keyboard and architectural drawings filled the screen. "I found them in the archives of the local city hall. The Swiss are obsessive about keeping records."

The drawings showed three separate chapels, a grand ballroom, a large room that was probably for dining, a drawing room and library and many smaller rooms on the ground floor. A sweeping staircase led to the upper stories. Servant's stairs were hidden away out of sight of the main rooms. A maze of concealed passages went behind the walls, allowing servants to move about the house unobtrusively, where they wouldn't annoy the nobility. Steps led down from a huge kitchen to arched vaults of stone built under the château.

"You can see how they built that wall to keep the river out." Stephanie used a laser pointer to indicate what she was talking about. "The vaults are perfect for storing wine and food. The temperature would be cool, constant in summer or winter."

Stephanie tapped a key. The monitor switched to a moving video in color.

"This is a video taken by a cruise ship line that goes up and down the river. Gutenberg's château is ideal from an advertising point of view because it's a beautiful example of old European architecture. I thought you might see something useful."

They watched as the video moved past the château. The remains of a crumbling dock stuck out into the river from a narrow shelf next to the wall. Set in the wall at the end of the dock was a rusted metal door. The door looked old and immovable. The château looked romantic and picturesque.

"That door doesn't look like it's been opened for a hundred years," Nick said.

"Where does it go?" Selena asked.

Stephanie brought up the drawing. "Into the vaults. They would have used it to unload fresh produce and goods from the river."

"That's our way in," Ronnie said. "We can't go in through the front. The fake delivery or repairman bit won't fly here."

"I wish we had more Intel," Nick said.

"There's never enough Intel. Besides, think of all the times when the Intel we had was wrong."

"Yeah, but that doesn't stop me from wishing we had more. Run the video again, will you Steph? I thought I saw something."

They watched as the château started to slip by.

"Hold it there," Nick said. The picture froze. "There. On top of the wall."

"I see it," Ronnie said.

"What are you looking at?" Selena asked.

"See that shiny line? The sun must've caught it just right when they were filming. You have to look close, it's really hard to see."

A shimmering, hair thin line ran along the top of the wall a few inches above the tips of the broken glass.

"Trip wire," Ronnie said. "If he's got that, he's got cameras and some kind of backup alarm system as well."

"I wonder how many guards he has," Selena said.

"More than we'd like," Nick said.

"There's always one guard at the gate," Stephanie said. "There's the chauffeur. Probably a dozen staff inside, but some of those would be noncombatants. Cooks, housekeepers, people like that."

"All that tells us is that we don't know how many are in there. With Krivi and Mitchell and the others gone, he has to be paranoid as hell. If I were him, I'd have armed men all around me."

"How do you want to play it?" Elizabeth asked. "We need to move before he sends someone else out with one of those canisters."

"Ronnie's right," Nick said. "We'll never get through that front gate."

"You want to try that door?" Ronnie asked.

"Right now it looks like the best shot," Nick said. "But if we have to blow it open it will alert everyone inside."

"We could go over the wall," Selena said. "That wire shouldn't be much of a problem."

"We could, but we'd be exposed on top. Gutenberg must have security cameras. We'd be sitting ducks up there and when we drop down, there's no cover until we reach the house. Time enough to send out the goons. It's a kill zone."

Ronnie said, "I can use the plasma cutter. It will go right through that old metal."

"How soon can you leave?" Elizabeth asked.

"Give us an hour to put our gear together," Nick said.

CHAPTER 60

The raft was a rental from a company in
Geneva that specialized in supplying whatever was
needed for tourists with a yen for seeing the Rhône
up close and personal. Clouds covered the moon.
The château was a dark mass looming out of the
night. In their black gear, the three of them were
just one more bit of darkness.

The raft bumped up against the rotting remains
of the old dock. Ronnie tied off and they climbed up
onto the flat area next to the wall of the château.
Nick shone a light on the rusted metal of the ancient
door. A metal plate in the center held a large
keyhole.

"Can you pick that lock?"

Ronnie peered into the keyhole. "It's solid rust.
Be quicker if I cut it away."

He took the plasma unit from his pack. It was
compact and self-contained, good for about twenty
minutes, long enough for most uses in the field.
Ronnie donned goggles, turned it on and began
cutting. The torch made a bright, blue flame,
showering sparks as he cut. The metal glowed red
on either side of the cut as he moved the beam
around the lock plate. After a few minutes he shut
down the torch and took off his goggles.

"That should do it."

He stood and used his knife to pry the plate
away from the door. It fell onto the ground.

"Give me a hand," Ronnie said.

Nick and Ronnie pulled on the door. Flakes of
rust broke away but it didn't move.

"Again," Nick said. This time they felt movement. "Once more should do it."

They pulled. The door came open with a screeching sound of tortured metal.

"They must've heard that in Geneva," Nick said.

"As long as they didn't hear it up top," Selena said. "Are we going in or not?"

They stepped into the lowest vault of the château and brought out their flashlights. The arched ceiling of the vault was made of fitted stones. The floor was of stone. Old barrels and crates and pieces of lumber littered the floor. A thick layer of dust lay over everything. A narrow flight of steps rose at the far end to the next level.

"No one's been here in a long time," Nick said. "I wonder if they even know that door is there."

"They will after we leave," Ronnie said.

"Let's climb. Weapons free."

They charged their MP-5s. The sound of the bolts going home echoed in the stone space.

The steps led to a closed wooden door. Nick pushed against it until it showed dim light from the room beyond. They opened it further and stepped into another vault. This one had been converted into a furnace room. Three low wattage bulbs hung from the ceiling, shedding light enough to see a modern gas fired boiler positioned against one wall. A four inch gas main descended from the ceiling to a large, spoked valve and then over to a meter and control console on the side of the boiler. The panel held more valves and several gauges. They could hear the low sound of the pilot light burning. Pipes rose from the boiler and branched out along the ceiling.

"That's a serious furnace," Ronnie said. "Look at the size of that gas line. I'd hate to see the heating bill."

"Gutenberg can afford it," Nick said. "The next level up should be the ground floor. I don't see steps."

"There's another vault through there," Selena said. She pointed at an open archway on the wall opposite the furnace. They headed over to it. Nick held up his hand.

Wait.

He took a quick look into the next room and signaled them forward.

They entered a wine cellar lit by dim, overhead bulbs. On one side, racks of wine and liquor bottles stood in dusty rows, five shelves high. A wide aisle ran down the middle of the vault, toward another set of steps leading upward. On the other side of the aisle stood a dozen round, steel cylinders, each about four feet high. Nick had seen cylinders like that before. They were the kind used by crop dusters.

He walked over to them. Each one was marked in red.

SR

Selena came up beside him. "SR. I'll bet it's short for Schwarze Rose, Black Rose. These are full of plague."

"Son of a bitch," Nick said.

"The bastard means to spray that stuff from the air," Ronnie said.

"This ends tonight," Nick said. His lips were pulled into a tight line.

He looked at the steps leading up from the wine cellar.

"If I remember those plans right, those steps lead to the kitchen."

"That makes sense," Selena said.

"Once we're inside it won't take long before they discover us. Anyone that's armed, shoot them. We don't know if there's any more of this stuff except what's down here, so don't kill Gutenberg. We have to try and take him alive."

The muffled sound of automatic weapons came through the closed door to the kitchen.

"What the hell is that?" Ronnie said. "Sounds like a firefight up there."

"Only one way to find out," Nick said.

CHAPTER 61

Albert Halifax settled back in the soft leather and sipped whisky from one of Gutenberg's collection of fine single malts. The glow of a Tiffany lamp on the end table cast a mellow light over his polished wing tip shoes. He was on his third drink. Across from him, Gutenberg sat with a similar glass in a similar chair, waiting for Halifax to come to the point.

The British Chancellor of the Exchequer had arrived unannounced earlier that afternoon, accompanied by his personal bodyguard. The two men sitting in Gutenberg's study were the last leaders of AEON.

Halifax broke the silence. "A thousand years and it comes to this."

"What do you mean, Albert?"

"You know what I mean. Centuries of work undone and all because of an upstart group of Americans no one seems able to eliminate. It reminds me of Shakespeare, done badly."

"Shakespeare?"

"Who will rid me of this turbulent priest?" Halifax quoted. "Richard the III." His voice was husky with the Scotch.

"It's not over yet, Albert."

"No?"

"No. Besides, it's not just the Americans. The Russians are responsible for most of the events of the past week."

"Russians, Americans, what's the difference? We're next."

"This isn't like you, Albert. Get hold of yourself." Gutenberg's voice took on an edge of steel. "You're safe here. Tomorrow the containers will be taken to the airfield. By the next day, the disease will be released over Moscow and New York and everyone will be too busy to worry about us. I should have done that in the first place instead of sending Schmidt. We only need to be patient a while longer."

"I can't say I'm sorry about Krivi," Halifax said. "Pushy wog. But I must admit, he was useful."

"Look at it this way. Albert. You and I now control all of AEON's resources. We'll find new men to take the place of the others and this time, we'll consolidate the power between the two of us. Lately things had become too..."

"Democratic?" Halifax finished for him.

"Yes, exactly."

Shouts sounded somewhere in the building. Then the sound of automatic weapons.

"What was that?" Halifax said.

Gutenberg stood. "Come with me."

Halifax rose as Gutenberg strode over to a wall of books. He reached up to the fourth shelf and tugged on a leather bound volume near the end. The bookcase swung open, revealing a lighted passage beyond.

The two men stepped inside. Gutenberg pulled on a lever and the bookcase slid shut. They were in a passage three feet wide, lit at intervals by bulbs overhead.

"You devil," Halifax said. "I haven't seen one of these servant passages in years."

"It's quite extensive. We can go anywhere on the first and second floors. There are peepholes in each room."

Intermittent gunfire sounded through the walls. The sounds were muted inside the passageway.

"This way," Gutenberg said.

They moved down the passage until they came to a corridor branching off to the right.

"What about stray rounds?" Halifax asked. His voice was nervous.

"We're safe in here. The walls are stone, nothing's coming through them."

Gutenberg stopped and peered through a small opening in the wall. A lever protruded from the wall. He pulled it down and a section of the wall opened into a dimly lit room. The sound of shooting was much louder.

"Where are we?" Halifax whispered.

"This is the gun room," Gutenberg said.

He went to a large glassed cabinet and opened it with a key he took from his vest pocket. One side of the cabinet held shotguns and rifles in an upright rack. The other side held a second, smaller cabinet with several drawers. Gutenberg pulled open the bottom drawer and took out a German Luger pistol and two loaded magazines. He inserted a magazine into the gun, pulled back on the toggle slide and stuck the pistol in his belt. He dropped the second magazine in his jacket pocket.

"This one's for you." Gutenberg handed Halifax a Walther .380. "It's loaded. I assume you know how to use it."

"Of course."

Halifax managed to sound offended. He reached around Gutenberg and took an engraved over and under shotgun from the rack.

"I prefer one of these."

Gutenberg shrugged. "As you will. Ammunition is right there."

Halifax loaded the gun. "Now what?"

"Now we find out what's happening. My men should have things under control by now."

A sudden burst of fire in the next room sent them scurrying back into the hidden passageway. The door closed behind them.

"That doesn't sound like it's under control," Halifax said.

"If you have nothing positive to say, keep quiet."

Without waiting for a reply, Gutenberg moved along the corridor and put his eye to the spy hole looking into the next room.

He saw two of his men lying on the floor. Both were dead. A man in gray battle dress and wearing a red beret stood over one of the bodies. Gutenberg recognized the insignia on his collar.

"Russians," he hissed under his breath.

"Russians? Why would they be here?"

"They're after me," Gutenberg said. "And if they know you're here, they're after you too."

"What shall we do?"

"Nothing. We wait until they decide we're not here and go away."

The shooting had stopped.

"You might as well get comfortable," Gutenberg said.

CHAPTER 62

Nick waited at the head of the stairs by the kitchen door. Ronnie and Selena were on the steps behind him.

"Ready?"

He pushed the door open. It moved a few inches and lodged against something soft and heavy. Nick looked through the opening and saw part of a brightly lit kitchen counter. A rack of metal pots hung over it. The shooting had died out. He pushed harder until the door was open enough to slip through. The body of a large man in a white apron and shirt had been blocking the door. His shirt was red with blood. A large knife lay near his hand. Vegetables were scattered over the floor.

"They shot the cook," Selena said. "Why do that?"

"He's a witness," Nick said. "Whoever it is, they're not going to leave anyone alive in this building."

"They must be after Gutenberg, just like we are," Ronnie said.

"Yeah. You thinking what I'm thinking?"

"Russians?" Ronnie said.

"Probably Spetsnaz. Vysotsky's people."

"How many you think?"

"Not too many. Maybe eight or ten. They wouldn't need more than that."

Nick led them over to where the kitchen doors stood open to the rest of the Château.

"Too bad Korov isn't here," Ronnie said. "We might get by without shooting it out."

"You want to try and convince them we're on their side?" Nick said.

"Nah. Just sayin'."

Nick turned to Selena.

"You see movement, don't hesitate. Shoot it."

"What if it's someone like the cook? Not one of the Russians or Gutenberg's men?"

"Hear that?" Nick asked.

"Hear what? It's quiet."

"Exactly. The shooting's over. They've killed everyone they came across. You see someone, they're an enemy. Take them down."

She nodded.

"They don't know we're here. If I were them, I'd be headed this way to check out those vaults. I don't want to get stuck in this kitchen. We'll take it to them."

The doors from the kitchen opened onto a wide hall and staging area with tables where dishes could be set before being taken to the dining room. To the left of the staging area, stairs led up to the second level. To the right, the space was taken up by storage closets. Straight ahead, the passage continued toward the rest of the ground floor. Another body lay facedown beyond the tables. He was dressed in a suit. The stock of an assault rifle stuck out from under his body. His blood made a wide red pool on the floor.

One of Gutenberg's guards, Nick thought.

They moved past the body and took up positions on either side of the opening where the hall moved on into the rest of the building. Voices sounded ahead, coming closer. They were speaking Russian. Nick held up three fingers and mouthed *on three.*

One. Two. Three.

On three, they leaned around the doorjamb and opened fire.

The first thing Selena saw was three men in gray battle dress and red berets. They carried short barreled assault rifles that looked ugly and efficient. The bullets knocked them down before they had a chance to raise the rifles. Out of sight in an adjoining passage, Selena heard someone start shouting in Russian.

Ronnie took a grenade from his belt, pulled the pin and hurled it down the passage. They ducked back. The grenade detonated and Nick ran forward into the hall. Without thinking, Selena followed. Someone looked around a corner and fired. The rounds whistled by as Nick shot him. She sensed Ronnie pounding along the hall behind her. She felt invincible, strong, adrenaline punching through her veins.

They passed the spot where the grenade had gone off. The walls and floor and ceiling were spattered with blood. Two bodies lay on the floor, blown apart by the grenade. At least she thought it was two. It was hard to tell.

Behind the wall, Gutenberg watched them go by. He recognized Carter.

Those are the people who have been causing so much trouble, he thought. *Well, they won't be doing it for much longer.*

The dining room had a long, polished mahogany table with a gleaming crystal chandelier hanging over it. Vysotsky's men opened fire as Selena started into the room. Bullets ripped into a half dozen oil paintings hung on the wall behind her. A round slammed into her vest and knocked her back into the hall and onto the floor. She gasped for air.

Ronnie and Nick fired into the room. The chandelier exploded into glittering fragments. The noise of the guns was deafening. A door opened on the opposite side of the hall. She rolled to her side and fired at the opening. Someone screamed and fell back into the room.

Then it was over.

The hallway stank of burnt powder and hot metal. The coppery scent of fresh blood seeped into the air. Nick came over to her.

"Give me a hand," she said.

He helped her to her feet. "You're okay?"

"It just knocked the wind out of me. I'm fine."

"I make it nine dead Russians," Ronnie said.

"That figures. Eight enlisted and one officer," Nick said.

"We still haven't found Gutenberg."

"He's probably hiding."

Somewhere a door closed.

"You hear that?" Ronnie said. "It sounded like it came from the kitchen."

They ran back the way they had come and into the kitchen. The body of the cook still lay on the floor. The door to the vault was closed.

"Didn't we leave that open?" Selena asked.

Nick nodded. "Somehow Gutenberg must've gotten past us and gone down into the vault."

"Bad move," Ronnie said. "He's trapped."

"Yeah. Maybe. Or maybe not. Why hide where he can't get away?"

"There could be another way out," Selena said. "Something we didn't see when we were down there."

"Only one way to find out," Nick said. "Let's go see."

In the vault beneath the kitchen, Gutenberg and Halifax stood in front of a tall wine rack.

"Help me empty this," Gutenberg said.

He began pulling bottles off the rack, two and three at a time. They shattered on the stone floor, splashing wine onto his dove gray slacks.

Halifax said, "My dear man, this is hardly the time for a glass of wine."

"Don't be an idiot, Albert. There's an old tunnel behind this that will take us outside the walls. This isn't the first time the château has been under siege. Now, give me a hand."

The two men began throwing bottles onto the floor. The wine spread in a growing pool around their feet. Soon the heavy wine rack was light enough to move. They pulled it away from the wall, revealing a dark, wooden door.

A rusted, iron ring hung from the middle of the door. Gutenberg took hold of the ring and pulled. With difficulty, it began to come open.

CHAPTER 63

Nick came down the steps, MP-5 held close by his cheek. He heard something scraping across the floor. He reached the bottom of the steps and saw Gutenberg and another man in front of a door set into the wall of the vault.

"It's all done, Gutenberg. Stop what you're doing."

Gutenberg froze. He turned toward Nick and raised his pistol. But he wasn't pointing at Nick and the others. The gun was aimed at the rows of steel containers.

"I wouldn't advise you to shoot," Gutenberg said. "Bullets will ricochet in here from the stone walls. If one of them hits any of those containers, you are all dead. It will take a week or so before they put your rotting, blackened body into the ground, but you'll still be dead. If you make one move toward me I'll fire."

"Nick, he means it," Selena said. "He's crazy."

Gutenberg heard her and laughed. "Crazy? I'm not the one who's crazy. It's people like you."

Ronnie whispered in Nick's ear. "I can take him. Let me take the shot."

"Don't try it," Gutenberg said.

"Looks like we have a stalemate," Nick said. "You know I can't let you go."

"You don't have a choice. I really will shoot, you know. Let me make a proposal."

Beside Gutenberg, Halifax started breathing heavily. He raised his hand and began rubbing his chest.

"Humor him, Nick." Selena's voice was quiet.

"I'm listening," Nick said. "What did you have in mind?"

On the side of the room, the big boiler fired up. The flames made a low, steady roar in the background.

"We're going into this tunnel," Gutenberg said.

Halifax clutched his chest. He gave a strangled cry, dropped his shotgun and fell against Gutenberg. The shotgun struck the floor and went off. The blast struck the big meter feeding gas to the boiler furnace. Gas poured out with a loud hissing sound. Ronnie fired at Gutenberg and hit him in the shoulder, sending his pistol flying. Gutenberg cursed and ducked behind the wooden door and pulled it shut behind him. They heard a bar fall into place on the other side.

The air in the vault stank of escaping gas.

"We have to get out of here," Nick said. "That gas will blow and we can't do anything about it."

"Which way?" Selena asked. She coughed.

"The way we came in. It's the quickest way out."

They ran to the stairs leading to the lower vault and scrambled down them. Fresh air blew in from the river, clearing away the cloud of gas that followed them. They went through the old door. The moon had come out, shining pale silver light over the river. Their raft was tied where they'd left it. They clambered in and paddled hard, away from the château. They'd reached the middle of the river before the gas exploded.

The sound was like deep thunder inside a mountain. A billowing gust of flame shot out of the open door in the lower vault. The retaining wall blew outward into the river, sending stones splashing into the water just yards away from where they fought to put distance between themselves and the building. Waves rocked the raft.

"Whoa," Ronnie said. "Look at that."

The foundation had been undermined by the explosion. The back wall of the building collapsed in slow motion and dropped into the water with an ominous grinding sound. Plumes of water fountained into the air and rained down around them.

One of the tall towers began to lean.

"The whole building is going," Selena said. "The vaults must have been destroyed. They were holding everything up."

The tower toppled onto the roof. A second tower crumbled, then the roof fell inward and the building collapsed upon itself. The noise was unlike anything Nick had ever heard. A great cloud of white dust rose into the moonlit night. The rumbling and grinding of stone went on for what seemed like a long time before the sounds died away.

The château was gone. Only the outer walls remained.

"Gutenberg," Selena said.

"He was under all that. He has to be dead. Keep paddling. Don't forget those cylinders full of plague were in there."

"They must have been wiped out by the explosion," Ronnie said. "The fire would have burned off anything that got released."

"Probably, but I don't want to wait and find out the hard way that it wasn't."

They paddled downstream until they came to the narrow cove they'd used to launch into the water. Their rented van was hidden under the trees nearby.

"What about the raft?" Selena asked.

"Leave it. We don't have time to pack it up. We need to get away from here. Get changed."

They changed into civilian clothes. The weapons and gear went into an aluminum case. Their diplomatic passports would get them past inspection and back to their plane, waiting in Geneva.

CHAPTER 64

Nick sat in the comfort of a wide leather armchair in the forward cabin of the Gulfstream, sipping an Irish whiskey. They were two hours out of Switzerland, headed back to Washington. He could feel the tension leave his shoulders as Ireland's magic began working.

Selena sat next to him, head back and eyes closed, asleep. Ronnie was in a chair across the aisle, reading a magazine.

He thought about everything that had happened in the last few weeks. It was a blur. He thought about Adam and wished he could tell him that AEON was finally finished. Even though he'd never known his real identity, in some way Adam had become a friend.

Nick thought about the people he'd seen dying in agony in Brazil. He hadn't been able to stop that from happening, but they'd kept Gutenberg from carrying out his plan to kill millions more. An evil man. If there was a hell, Nick hoped Gutenberg was in it. It was what he deserved.

He raised his glass. "Pretty good work," he said.

"What is?" Selena was awake. She yawned.

"Stopping Gutenberg. I was just thinking about what an evil bastard he was. We stopped him. Like I said, pretty good work."

"Pour me a drink."

Nick took ice from a bucket by his chair, added it to a fresh glass and filled it with whiskey.

"Here you go," he said.

"To good work," she said.

They drank.

"This one was hard," she said.

"They're all hard."

Selena looked out the window. "How are we going to replace Lamont?"

"It won't be easy but Harker will find someone. It's going to be a tough adjustment."

"How much longer do you think we can do this?" she asked.

"You miss your old life?"

"Some of it. I miss seeing students get excited about learning but I don't miss stuffy faculty parties and self-important professors who want to argue with me. After the last couple of years I could never go back to that. It would seem terribly boring."

Nick laughed. "Yeah, you can't say that what we do is boring."

"Do you think AEON is finally out of our lives?"

"I think so. But there's always someone out there who believes the world exists for their personal exploitation. It won't be long until something else like AEON comes along."

"That's a depressing thought."

"It's always been that way, all through history. The people who run things never learn."

Selena looked out the window. Dawn revealed the gray waters of the Atlantic far below.

"What am I going to do about my sister?" she said.

Her question took him by surprise.

"There's not much you can do. She's not really your sister, even though she has your father's blood."

"Yes she is, as much as I don't want to admit it. I wonder if she knows about me?"

"If Vysotsky has anything to say about it, I don't think she does," Nick said. "You'd be just as much of a surprise to her as she was to you."

"I wonder if we'll ever meet?"

"That might not be a great idea. Don't forget who she works for and what she does."

"I don't think there's much of a chance I'll forget that."

Nick changed the subject.

"I'm looking forward to getting back."

"So am I. I want to start putting our new place together."

"You just want to go shopping."

"Jerk." She punched him in the shoulder. "Seriously, aren't you excited about it?"

"About shopping? No. But I'm looking forward to living there with you."

"You are?"

Nick took her hand. "Yes. It took a while but I finally figured it out."

She looked at him. "Figured what out?"

"That we're a team," he said.

CHAPTER 65

Nick, Selena and Ronnie were in Elizabeth's office.

"Are you sure Gutenberg didn't get away?" Elizabeth asked.

"I don't see how he could have," Nick said. "There wasn't time for him to get very far and he was wounded. The building came down fast. It would have crushed him underneath."

Elizabeth nodded, once.

"The containers of plague were destroyed," Nick said, "but there could still be samples around. We never went into Krivi's corporate building to check the labs there."

"It's handled. Langley sent a team in. They recovered samples of the bacteria and two hundred vials of vaccine. We have what we need to stop the spread, once it's in production."

"How many have died?" Selena asked.

"I don't know the exact figure, but at least twenty-five thousand so far. There'll be more before it's done. It's still spreading. The borders of Brazil are closed and the entire country is under quarantine. It's wrecking their economy."

"So AEON wins after all," Nick said.

"Not quite. Aid is pouring in from all over the world. It seems not everyone in power thinks knocking out Brazil is a good idea. Don't forget, you stopped them from releasing the plague here. If Gutenberg had succeeded, millions would have died before a vaccination program was put in place."

"What about the Russians?" Selena said.

"What about them?"

"They could still have some samples."

"They might. If they do, they'll add it to their biological weapons inventory. Just like us."

Selena looked shocked.

"Us?"

"We'll store it with the other bio weapons we have."

"I thought all of that was illegal."

"It is. Technically speaking, we don't have biological weapons. We only have research facilities and samples stored for the purpose of creating vaccines and preventive measures."

"Yeah, right," Ronnie said.

"It's part of the MAD policy," Elizabeth said. "Mutual Assured Destruction. If our enemies know we have the capability to retaliate in kind against a biological attack, they might think twice about launching one against us."

"It's insane," Selena said, "immoral."

"But necessary. War has nothing to do with morality."

"Why did Vysotsky go after AEON?" Nick asked.

"It's not hard to understand," Elizabeth said. "It was Vysotsky's men who lost the samples in the first place. As far as the Kremlin was concerned, it was his fault and it was up to him to correct the problem. I think there was another element as well. From what I know of him, Alexei would take the deaths of his men as a personal insult. He's not a man to let an insult go by. He wanted revenge. Not to mention the fact that AEON posed a direct threat to the Federation."

"Does the president know about Senator Mitchell?"

"I intend to brief him later today. He needs to know so he can discover what Mitchell was doing. Whatever it was, you can be sure it wasn't in our interests."

"What are we going to do about Vysotsky?" Selena asked.

Elizabeth looked at her.

"Nothing. What would you have us do?"

"He sent my sister over here to kill an American senator. I know Mitchell was part of AEON but..."

"Selena. There's nothing we can do."

Selena opened her mouth to speak and closed it again.

Elizabeth reached into a drawer and took out several file folders.

"Nick, these are service records. Lamont's made it official. He's leaving at the end of the month and we need to replace him. I want you and Selena and Ronnie to look at possible candidates."

Nick reached over and took the files from her.

"It's not going to be the same without Lamont."

"No, but we don't have a choice."

"We'll get on it."

"That's all for today," Elizabeth said. "I just want to say that I'm glad you all made it back. Good work."

"We get a break?" Ronnie said.

"Count on a week unless something comes up."

Nick stood. "Come on, Selena. Let's go buy some furniture."

Elizabeth watched them leave and wondered how much longer the team would hold together. They were old for the kind of missions she sent them on. Ancient, by the standards of modern combat. Somehow they kept pulling it off. Lamont had been lucky, if you could call being left with a permanent limp lucky.

She got up and walked over to the counter with the coffee. It was the fuel that kept her going. She poured a cup and watched steam rise from the surface. She blew on the hot liquid to cool it and looked out through the bulletproof glass of the French doors at the patio and flowers that provided an illusion of normalcy.

AEON was finished, at least she hoped it was. Everything indicated that it was. But Elizabeth had learned that when one threat was finished, another waited in the wings. She opened the patio doors and took the coffee outside into the sunshine.

There would be time enough tomorrow to worry about what would come next.

New Releases...

Be the first to know when I have a new book coming out by subscribing to my newsletter. No spam or busy emails, only a brief announcement now and then. Just click on the link below. You can unsubscribe at any time...

http://alexlukeman.com/contact.html#newsletter

The Project Series: In Order

White Jade
The Lance
The Seventh Pillar
Black Harvest
The Tesla Secret
The Nostradamus File
The Ajax Protocol
The Eye of Shiva
Black Rose

Book 10 of the Project series, *King Solomon's Tomb*, is coming soon...

Reviews and comments by readers are welcome!

You can contact me at: alex@alexlukeman.com.
I promise to get back to you.

My website is: www.alexlukeman.com

Acknowledgements

As always, my wife Gayle. She soothes the troubled waters when I feel like dumping everything halfway through and starting over.

Neil Jackson, who designs the dynamite covers for the Project series and always goes the extra mile.

Special thanks to Nancy Witt, Susan Blanker, Seth Ballard, Eric Vollebregt and Paul Madsen.

Notes

Bubonic plague is one of the great scourges of mankind, bringing down empires and kings with murderous indifference. Over the millennia there have been several distinct variations, each different from the last. The Plague of Justinian swept through the Eastern Roman Empire in 541-42 CE and devastated the world from the Mediterranean to China.

A characteristic of the Plague of Justinian was blackening of the toes and fingers. It died out, as plagues do, only to reemerge again and again over the next three hundred years until it finally disappeared sometime in the ninth century. It is estimated that over one hundred million people died before it was done. That was in a world with a much smaller population than today. Imagine what would happen now, if a variation were to appear that couldn't be stopped by modern antibiotics.

Victims of the plague were recently unearthed in Egypt and their genomes extracted.

22932640R00166

Made in the USA
San Bernardino, CA
27 July 2015